THE SWITCHBACK TRAIL

Other Available Books by Terrell L. Bowers:

Judgment at Gold Butte
Destiny at Broken Spoke
Crossfire at Broken Spoke
Gun Law at Broken Spoke
Feud at Broken Spoke
Noose at Sundown

THE SWITCHBACK TRAIL

•

Terrell L. Bowers

AVALON BOOKS

NEW YORK

Published by Thomas Bouregy & Co., Inc.
160 Madison Avenue, New York, NY 10016

Library of Congress Cataloging-in-Publication Data

Bowers, Terrell L.
  The Switchback Trail / Terrell L. Bowers.
        p. cm.
    ISBN 978-0-8034-7781-0
  1. Ranchers—Fiction.   2. Murder—Fiction.   I. Title.
  PS3552.O87324S95 2010
  813'.54—dc22

                                        2010006235

PRINTED IN THE UNITED STATES OF AMERICA
ON ACID-FREE PAPER
BY HADDON CRAFTSMEN, BLOOMSBURG, PENNSYLVANIA

To Kyle

Prologue

Don Sanson was digging a posthole when the rider appeared. He paused to mop his brow as the visitor rode up and stopped his horse.

"Howdy," the man offered. "Looks like hard work."

Don returned his ready smile. "You can say that again."

"You're not putting in a whole section of fence by yourself, are you?" the new arrival asked. "It looks like a job for a dozen men."

Don laughed. "I only have three hired hands, other than during roundup, and they're moving the herd today. Once they finish up, they'll be along to lend a hand."

"I reckon it's good to keep busy," the rider said. "I heard about your wife. It must be lonely around the ranch without her."

That sobered Don's mood. "It comes on in the evenings, being lonesome, but not so much when there's work to be done. How did you know about my wife?"

"I'm new around town, but one of the fellows at the saloon told me about your run of bad luck. Some kind

1

of disease wiped out half your herd last year, and then your wife passed. I can see how that would knock a man to his knees."

Don mustered a grim smile. "Once on his knees, a righteous man uses such a time to pray."

The stranger gave a nod of agreement before asking, "I wonder if you might be interested in selling off your southern pasture. It would help pay for a bad year."

"The herd is doing better, now that the sickness is past."

"I'd wager you could get a good price for that land, being it controls the water along Wandering Creek for close to half a mile."

"No one controls the creek. It's there for my cattle and also provides water for a dozen or so farms down the valley." He lifted one shoulder in a shrug. "Plus the Melbourne place is upstream, so they have first access to the creek. If anyone was going to seize control of it, they would be the ones who have the water rights."

"What about the other ranch in the valley— Vanderpool? How is he supposed to get to the creek?"

"His cattle are able to get to water downstream. It's a bit of a chore for his beef, but he arrived in the valley last."

"It's like I was saying, you and Melbourne have the prime locations in the valley. I'd be willing to offer you a premium price for your southern range. Name your price. How about it?"

"We might as well be talking about sprouting wings and flying, my friend," Don said, no longer interested in discussing the subject. "I took out a mortgage on my ranch this past year so I could hold on to what land I've got. I'm not of a mind to sell a single foot of property."

The rider accepted his decision without further debate, removing his hat to fan his face. "Whew! It's a real scorcher today," he said, lowering the hat to his lap. "I hope your heart don't give out from too much sun."

Don chuckled. "I'm used to the sun and hard work. The last thing worrying me is heat stroke. I've got the heart of a lion."

Suddenly, the rider lifted the hat with his left hand. He had drawn his gun with his right, and it was pointed right at Don's chest.

Don took a step back but had no time to react. The sound of the shot cracked the stillness of the afternoon, but Don was too stunned to hear it. A white-hot missile passed through the left side of his chest, and every sensation was lost.

"A bullet stops even a lion's heart," the man's cold voice stated. "You should have listened to reason."

Don didn't realize he had fallen onto his back until he discovered the sun shining directly into his eyes. Funny, it was not the blinding light he had thought, but more of a dim glow. A last moment of reason warned him that his life was at an end. He moved his lips, trying to speak the Lord's Prayer, but the air had left his lungs. The living being who had been Don Sanson was no more.

The rider did not bother to get down and check his victim. He knew his aim was true. With not so much as a backward glance, he swung his horse about and rode away.

Chapter One

Cully Lomax had just finished greasing the axles on the carriage when he heard deliberate steps approach from behind him. Without turning to look, he knew the sound of those diminutive but smartly stamping feet. He wondered what new crisis demanded his immediate attention. If it wasn't Victoria needing a chaperone or driver, it was her mother, frantic that he drop whatever he was doing and help with a chore or run an errand.

Cully had reached the burn-out point with his old profession, exhausted from endless stress and dangerous work. When he was offered a job on the Melbourne ranch, it had sounded slow-paced and free of anxiety, the type of extended rest for which Cully had been searching. How tough could it be, doing the job of a handyman on a ranch? Minimal supervision, working daylight hours, with three meals a day and a roof over his head. No real responsibilities, no worries—simply follow orders, and unwind each evening after work. However, Jeff Melbourne had conveniently forgotten to mention the two querulous females who lived on the ranch. After six months around the place, Cully had done duty as escort, butler, and driver and been witness to many nonstop arguments and battles between the two Melbourne women.

"Cullen!" Victoria's voice was particularly shrill this morning. "Aren't you about finished with the runabout? I told you at breakfast that I would need the buggy today."

He recognized that the young woman was bubbling at the surface, a volcano primed to erupt, but with a tone of voice that was forever tactful and patient he said, "The singletree was cracked, so I had to attach hooks to a new one. Soon as I check the harness, you ought to be ready to go."

"Good!" She didn't conceal her impatience. "I have to get out of here before I . . ." She opened and closed her hands, making tight little fists. ". . . before I kill someone." Then, with a burning gaze on him, she snapped, "If you keep me waiting, it might just be you!"

"I'm nearly finished."

"My things are on the porch. Harness Mrs. Butters to the runabout, then pull up to the porch and stow everything aboard."

He arched his back to relieve the stiffness from bending over and used a clean cloth to wipe the grease from his hands. Glancing past the girl toward the house, he spied a picture that summoned hackles to rise at the back of his neck. Victoria's mother was framed in the doorway, hands on her hips, jaw thrust out defiantly. Stacked on the porch were a suitcase, blankets, and a bundle he recognized as being rolled-up canvas for a tent.

"What's going on, your mother finally drive you out of the house?"

"I'm going to visit my brother." Victoria bore into him with a smoldering gaze. "At least, I will if you ever get my transportation ready!"

"You're going on holiday?" He was incredulous. "I thought you were in the middle of planning the details of your upcoming marriage. It's only a few weeks away."

"How considerate of you to remind me of my personal agenda, Cullen." Victoria sneered haughtily. "My goodness! The wedding! It almost slipped my mind!"

He glanced skyward at a thick formation of dark clouds covering the distant horizon. "The weather doesn't look good for traveling. I'd say we're in for a storm tonight."

"So I'll pack a rain slicker. I'd rather be buried in mud up to my chin than attend my mother's party tomorrow night. She wants to display me like the prize horse at an auction."

"I get the feeling you're not exactly chomping at the bit to become Mrs. Winston Vanderpool."

"My future is no concern of yours," she retorted with a disdainful lilt. "I hardly think you are qualified to judge whom I should wed."

He grinned at her spunk. "Do tell."

"Look in the mirror sometime," she retorted. "You're a no-account cowboy, one of the nonachievers in life, an aimless vagabond, a lowly handyman! A drifter like you couldn't possibly know about taking responsibility or standing up to obligations for the sake of your family!"

He wondered why the word *obligation* had come up. Was there more to the wedding than the two most prominent single people in the valley getting married? He grinned insolently. "You've obviously given my character some thought. I'm right proud to think you've taken such an interest in me."

"You're dreaming if you think I have any interest in you!"

"Speaking of dreams," he said easily, "one day we should talk about the huge difference between the *you* in my dreams and *you* in person. There might be room for some compromise."

"I'm not concerned about your dumb dreams."

"See? That's what I mean. You're a much nicer person in my dreams."

"You may indulge your fantasies on your own time, Mr. Lomax." Victoria stretched out an arm and pointed to the porch. "I want Mrs. Butters in harness and the buggy at the door in five minutes!"

Cully ignored the demand while evaluating Victoria for a moment. As striking as a pixie, with perfectly sculptured features and an adequately proportioned body, she was a true beauty. Of course, the engaging looks were a part of her upbringing, as her mother had fashioned her for a privileged life. Raised with poise and grace, she had been educated and cajoled all of her life to act like royalty. He knew from experience that she was a much nicer human being when her mother wasn't around.

"Well?" she prompted him.

"Well, what?"

"What are you waiting for?"

"I'll get right on it," he said, returning to the present and carefully removing the last of the grime from his hands. "I wouldn't want to leave a dirty print on any of your belongings."

"How very thoughtful." Her voice oozed sarcasm. "And here I suspected you were purposely taking your own sweet time just to annoy me."

"You seem in an awful hurry."

"Actually, I wanted to leave before my hair turned gray."

Cully could feel the glower from Mrs. Melbourne all the way across the yard. A glance told him there was more than a little disharmony on the ranch today. His own opinion was that Martha should have been the one to marry Winston's father. They were a perfect match. Both belonged in Boston or upstate New York, wherever it was that snobs enjoyed rubbing elbows with other blue bloods and putting on airs. Jeff was too much an ordinary rancher. Victoria . . . well, she didn't exactly belong in either world. She had been conditioned to display pretentious charm and manners, but there was also a substantive and genuine side to her.

"Why are you looking at me like that?" Victoria wanted to know.

Cully hadn't realized he was staring. He immediately conjured up an easy grin.

"Why, ma'am' "—he again used a patient drawl—"it's because I so enjoy seeing the fire in your eyes. You have the most endearing way of looking at a man . . . kind of like he was something you picked up on your Sunday shoes whilst crossing the cow pasture."

"You shouldn't attempt to be a wit, Cullen," she quipped, "not when you're only half-qualified."

He chuckled, aware of how it infuriated her whenever he refused to take her insults seriously. "I thank you for the advice, ma'am. It's a relief to know you can actually have an opinion—without asking your mother."

The remark obviously stung her pride, and she lifted her chin rebelliously. "Are you going to continue to leer at me like some vulgar drunk, or are you going to do as you were told?"

"Hmm, hold on a moment. I should ponder those two options." He removed his worn, flat-crowned hat and scratched his head. "Us half-wits have a real chore when it comes to making big decisions."

"I don't know why I try to be civil to you," she declared, exasperation heating her words. "You're the most impudent, insulting, and rude handyman we ever hired!"

"Can't expect much from a low-life, nonachieving drifter," he replied, using her previous description of him, "Especially when I'm so overwhelmed by the beauty and charm of such a highborn lady as you."

"If I'm not pulling out of this yard in five minutes," she warned, "you're going to be looking for a new job! Is that on a base enough level for you to understand?"

"Yes, ma'am," Cully acquiesced, pretending he actually feared she would follow through with such a threat. "I'll get right to it. You only had to mention you were in a hurry."

He quickly went to the corral and caught up the mare Victoria called Mrs. Butters. She was a stout, gentle horse, getting along in years, but she was broke to harness, as well as for riding. He hitched her up quickly, jumped into the carriage, and pulled it over to the front of the house. Victoria had waited impatiently and then followed on foot. Cully hopped down to load up her belongings, but the explosion between mother and daughter began as soon as Victoria was within screaming distance.

"You can't do this, Victoria!" Martha Melbourne sounded about one breath from apoplexy. "I won't allow it! I won't!"

"Please, Mother, we've been through this. I need some time to myself. Rehearsals will begin in a couple more weeks. This is the last chance I'll have to visit Avery."

"I insist you take the stage to his inn."

"It's ten miles to town, and the stage only goes that way once each week."

Martha did not give up. "Then catch the train instead, and go to Cheyenne or Denver. You can stay at a nice hotel and do some shopping."

"I enjoy the solitude of the ride between here and Avery's inn. I can spend a night out under the stars and be there tomorrow."

"Neither your father nor I can go with you, and I won't have you making that long ride by yourself. What if you have an accident or get hurt?"

Victoria maintained an unyielding expression on her pert, youthful face. "I've been going to visit Avery every summer since he built the inn, Mother. I might never get to go again once I'm married to Winston."

"What about the party in Elk City tomorrow night? Everyone is expecting you!"

"If I'm off visiting, you'll just have to entertain the guests yourself." She bore into her mother with dark, nearly black, eyes. "After all, they're *your* friends, not mine."

"All right!" Martha conceded. "You needn't attend the party. But I still refuse to have you gallivanting forty miles over the hills by yourself."

"Mother, please. I need to get away. I really do."

"It's an insane idea! I won't allow it!" Martha appeared ready to explode. "What about bandits or Indians?"

"You know the Indians are all on reservations, and there's nothing between us and Avery but miles and miles of empty desert."

"That buggy is ten years old, and the mare is older than that. What if you break down, or the horse comes up lame? What if you fall and hurt yourself? You might be bitten by a snake! What if you get stuck somewhere—you admit that hardly any travelers ever take that old trail anymore."

"I can take care of myself."

The door opened behind Martha, and Jeff Melbourne emerged from the house. He was thin and frail, still weakened from a near-fatal stroke a year earlier. The left side of his body had not fully recovered, but he managed to get around with only a slight limp. He had obviously overheard the commotion.

"Jefford"—Martha whirled on him—"tell your daughter she is to stay home!"

"Daddy!" Victoria pleaded her own case at once. "I want to visit Avery and spend some time on my own. I'll be back in four days. Please!"

Jeff held up a bony hand to stop the bickering. "I believe we can reach some sort of an agreement," he said quietly.

Both women waited impatiently for him to continue. Martha was the head of the family in almost every category. Seldom did Jeff get between the two of them during an argument, but when he did step in, both of them accepted his word as final.

"You know about the party at the Social Center tomorrow night," Martha reminded him curtly. "I've already told her she didn't have to attend."

"It's mostly your social group," Jeff summarized, "and it wasn't arranged specifically for Victoria's benefit anyway."

"Yes, but this idea of—"

"I need to do this, Daddy!" Victoria cut her mother off quickly. "Please don't forbid me to visit Avery. I'll be fine."

"As I was about to suggest," Jeff began again, "it would be worrisome to your mother and me to have you make that long trip by yourself, daughter."

"Daddy, I . . ."

"But"—he raised his hand a second time to stop her objection—"I do understand your desire to get away and visit Avery. I know the pressure and tension of the upcoming wedding must be tremendous."

"Yes, Daddy, it is."

He looked past her to the carriage. "The old buggy is not the most reliable of transportation anymore. What if you break down?"

"Cullen has gone over it from tip to top," she countered.

He cast a glance at the distant clouds and gave a negative shake of his head. "It looks as if a storm is brewing. That trail can be a treacherous ride under the best of conditions."

"I'll be careful," Victoria insisted. "I'm sure Mrs. Butters and the runabout will be fine."

Jeff appeared to give the trip a thorough deliberation. Both women were watching, each anxious as to his decision. Finally he nodded his graying head. "I don't see any real harm in your going to visit Avery, Victoria. . . ."

"Oh, thank you, Daddy!" she cried.

"Jefford!" Martha shouted in alarm. "You can't be serious!"

This time he raised both frail hands to stop further debate. "You can go visit, Victoria," he repeated, but then added, "on the condition that Cullen goes with you."

"No!" Victoria instantly screamed her frustration. "No, no, *no!*"

He stood firm, unmoved by her outburst. "You can't make it to Avery's place in a single day, meaning you will have to spend tonight out on the prairie. It would ease our minds to know you weren't all alone out there."

"But that's the whole idea," she cried, "to be by myself!"

"Cullen will see to it that you get plenty of time alone." He looked in his direction. "Won't you, Cullen?"

"Jeff . . ." Cully began a plea of his own, "I don't think . . ."

"A hired hand?" Martha was fuming. "Out in the middle of nowhere with Victoria—spending a night on the trail? Just the two of them? Jefford, that's not at all acceptable!"

"Daddy, it's not fair!" Victoria was equally incensed.

Jeff ignored both of their outbursts. "We can't risk having you roam out in the hills alone, Victoria. It's too dangerous. Too many things can happen."

"But I don't want to take some smart-mouthed handyman along!" Victoria shouted. "I don't need a nursemaid!"

Jeff stood his ground. "Either he goes with you, or you forget the whole idea."

"She ought to stay home where she belongs," Martha snapped. "I've given her everything a girl could ask for. Is this the reward I get for my years of sacrifice?"

"*Your* sacrifice?" Victoria wailed back. "Who is the one marrying Winston?"

Victoria and the older woman stared daggers at each other, two granite statues in a battle of wills, one that Cully knew the girl had lost at each and every confrontation in her life. Jeff's word would be the deciding factor.

So why punish me? he wondered. *I thought Jeff and I were friends. Now he stabs me in the back and twists the knife like a corkscrew!* He sighed in defeat, knowing he was destined to go on the trip with Jeff's daughter. In her irate mood, she would scald the hide right from his flesh. He would be the target of all of her anger and pent-up frustration.

"It's settled," Jeff said quietly, interrupting Cully's morbid assessment. "If the carriage should break down, Cully will be there to fix it. If need be, he can take the horse and ride for help. Those are the terms, Victoria. You can accept them, or you can stay home and attend the party tomorrow night with your mother."

Victoria shifted her smoldering glare from her mother, boring into Cully with eyes that were twin shards of ice. "All right." She fairly hissed the words. "I'm exhorted by my own father." With vehemence she added, "Get your gear, handyman. Five minutes—not one second more!"

Cully cast a desperate, inquisitive look at Jeff. To his dismay, the man had a rather satisfied look on his face. That made even less sense.

Maybe I only thought we were friends.

Chapter Two

Roy Weathers, the Elk City sheriff, looked around for hoofprints, but Don Sanson's three hired hands had already ridden their horses up to the fence line. Once they found their dead boss, one man had ridden for help, and another had gone back to the house and brought a blanket to cover the body. There had been so much going and coming, it was impossible to discern which horse had made which set of tracks.

"Think hard, boys." Roy coaxed. "Has anyone made a threat against Don lately?"

"You knew Don," one of the men replied. "Everyone liked him. He didn't have an enemy in the world."

"Who is next of kin?" the sheriff wanted to know.

"Don't have one," the same man replied. "His boy died from fever two or three years back, and his wife passed last winter from pneumonia. Far as I know, Don was all alone."

"He owe money to anyone?"

"Took a mortgage on the ranch after we lost about

half of the herd last year to the Texas fever, and he maybe owed a bit for supplies and such, but the place was still paying the bills."

"Cattle doing okay this year?"

"Healthy as can be, Sheriff. Don expected to have enough beef for the fall drive to pay the mortgage."

"All right, I'll speak to the banker and stop by the general store," Roy said, speaking more to himself than the three hired hands. "I'll need you boys to bring the body in for the doctor to look at. I reckon Don wanted to be buried next to his wife, here at the family cemetery."

"He told me as much at his wife's funeral," one ranch hand said. "Never figured that day would come so sudden."

Roy gave a nod. "One of you bring up a wagon so we can take Don to town. The other two might want to prepare his grave. I expect we'll bury him tomorrow. Soon as I get back to town, I'll pass the word and contact the parson. Once you dig Don's final resting place, you men get in touch with the nearby ranches and farms. . . . Let's say tomorrow afternoon for the service."

"What are we supposed to do after he's buried?" one of the men wanted to know. "The three of us have been working for Don for a number of years. He laid off the other hands when things went south last year. We have wages due, and the cattle still need someone to watch over them."

"I'll speak to Vanderpool at the bank. I'm sure he

will continue to pay you boys to keep the ranch going until someone else assumes control. I reckon anything beyond that will be betwixt you and the new owner."

"Guess that's the best we can hope for," the man replied. "Sure going to miss Don. He was the best man I ever worked for." Both of the others bobbed their heads in agreement.

Roy hesitated long enough to look around again. He was a fifty-year-old man who handled drunks on Saturday night, looked into petty crimes, or occasionally stopped a minor feud between neighbors. He had never had to investigate an actual murder. No witnesses, no motive, no clues—where the hell did a man start looking?

He waved a hand, as if shooing the three men into action. "Get started on the grave, and bring up the wagon. Let's get this over with."

Victoria held the reins tightly in her fists and drove the horse in silence, as dark and sullen as Cully had ever seen her.

"I'm saddled with you," she declared after a time, "but I want a few things clearly understood." She cast a stern glance at him. "First off, I don't want you speaking to me unless I initiate the conversation."

"No speaking," Cully repeated.

"Second, I don't want you spying on me either."

"No looking."

"And a third rule—don't be mimicking me!"

"Mimicking you?" he repeated, as if not understanding what she meant.

"Yes, repeating everything I say."

"No repeating everything you say," he teased.

Victoria heaved a sigh. "You're going to be a much bigger nuisance than I ever imagined."

He mustered a smirk. "I had no idea you had been imagining the two of us being together."

Victoria groaned. "I'm so going to hate having you along on this trip."

"If you noticed, it wasn't my idea to come along."

"What kind of hold do you have over my father?" she demanded petulantly. "Did you see him kill someone? Did you catch him branding someone else's cattle? And now you're using that knowledge to blackmail him? Why does he treat you like his best friend, rather than the rude, impertinent, hired hand you are?"

He scoffed at the notion. "You think his sending me with you was an act of friendship?"

"We had to let many of our riders go after the cattle sickness last year . . . yet he hired you."

"I'm handy to have around."

"It has to be more than that, although Dad says you can fix most anything. Where did you acquire such a complex background?"

"I picked up most of what I know doing odd jobs."

"Such as?"

"You know, robbing graves, building gallows, overseeing a ladies undergarment factory back east . . . the usual places a man picks up general knowledge."

"I don't believe a word of that."

"All right, I worked for a circus when I was a young

man." At her frown, he grinned. "But only until I got caught kissing the bearded lady." The furrow deepened in her brow as he finished the tall tale. "I would have stayed to fight for her, but she belonged to the carnival strongman. He could bend cast-iron bars using his teeth. I didn't want to have him bite off my ear or something."

"Gracious," she groaned, "you don't actually expect me to believe any of your ridiculous stories, do you?"

"Not really."

"So why concoct such exaggerated lies? Why not tell the truth?"

"The truth is boring. How interesting would it be if I were to admit that my father was a blacksmith and I was drafted into being his helper as a boy?"

"Is that the truth?"

"More or less."

"You're no kid, you have a fair amount of skill, and you speak like a modestly educated man, so what are you doing working at a nothing job for my father?"

"I heard that he had a sweet, angelic, beautiful daughter . . . fairest maid in all the land." At the compression of her lips, he smiled. "Sure hope I get to meet your sister one of these days."

"I'm an only child." She patiently played his game.

"Dad-gum!" he groaned, displaying a pained expression. "I went and hired out to the wrong guy!"

"Very funny."

"I can be at times," he retorted cheerfully.

"So make me laugh."

"Let's see. . . . When I was born, instead of slapping me on the bottom, my mother took one look at me and slapped my father." At her pinched eyebrows, he tried again. "I used to ride fence for a horse ranch, but I kept falling off."

She sighed, clearly unimpressed. "I could laugh at your lame attempts at humor, but I don't wish to encourage you to tell more bad jokes."

He studied her reaction. "Your marriage to Winston Vanderpool is about as bad a joke as I can imagine."

"You have no right to say that," she said tightly, an immediate flush of color rushing to her cheeks. "Winston is a refined gentleman."

"Yeah, he's so cultured, I'll bet he can bore a person on a dozen different subjects."

No comment came from Victoria.

"His best friend is the guy he sees in the mirror—the one he calls *handsome devil*," he tried again.

She still refused to budge, but her mouth drew into a tight line.

"If he wasn't pompous and incredibly boring, he'd have no personality at all."

"Enough already!" she exploded.

He chuckled. "I sure hope, when the day comes that I find the right girl, she jumps to my defense as quickly as you did for what's-his-name."

"Drop the subject, Cullen," she ordered. "My marrying Winston is none of your business."

He could tell she was serious, and he kept his silence. Victoria continued to direct the horse along a route that was not much more than a deer trail in spots, winding between trees, up steep banks, and through creek crossings. They ascended hill after hill, following the rolling terrain for miles. Cully took out his watch after they had been traveling for several hours. The sun was about an hour from sinking over the horizon.

"We going to travel all night?" he asked.

"We're about there."

"Your brother's place?"

"The halfway point," she replied.

"Seems a lot of trouble, riding fifty miles just to see your brother."

"He has always been my . . . confidant." She sighed. "I need to speak to him."

"And do you always spend a night on the trail when you visit?"

"I can make the ride in one day, but it means starting out at daybreak and continuing till well after dark. It's easier to break the trip into two days traveling. We'll camp next to the creek."

Victoria turned the runabout toward some low foothills, and they followed a trail that dipped through a deep wash, angled up a steep slope, and ended abruptly at a small clearing near the crest of a hill. She set the brake and lowered her head, as if meditating. Cully respected her moment of tranquility and waited patiently for her to give him an order.

"This is where I come when I need to be alone," she murmured, as if talking to herself. "It's beautiful and serene, totally quiet and peaceful. No one else in the world ever comes to this place. The only evidence of human existence is from my being here before. This is a private place . . . my private world."

"It is a long way from the nearest hint of civilization," Cully remarked.

The girl perked up at his words and cast a hard look at him. "Yes, that's the idea."

She climbed out of the buggy and pointed to a spot. "Erect my shelter on that flat place down next to the stream." Then she turned to him. "You can camp over the hill somewhere out of sight. I want to pretend you are a thousand miles away. I don't want to see or hear you. This might be my last visit to this place. I intend to spend as much time as I can and enjoy it . . . alone."

"No problem." He was agreeable. "You set down the rules, and I'll do my best to stick to them."

"The rules are simple. You pitch my tent, prepare the meal, and collect the firewood. Other than that, I don't want to know you're alive until we start for my brother's place tomorrow."

"You're the boss."

"Keep reminding yourself of that fact."

Cully walked over and scouted the area for putting up her tent. He discovered she had followed him and was standing a few feet away. "I want it right there," she said, indicating a low, flat section. "I like to go to sleep listening to the trickle of the brook."

He took a moment to survey the ravine. The walls along the entrance were smooth and perpendicular until the wash bellied out. It was open for a couple hundred feet, including the low area in which he was standing, before the creek narrowed like a funnel to pass through a rocky gorge. The stream then dipped out of sight, but he knew it wound around the side of the hill to where they had crossed it with the buggy, before continuing its path down to the flat country below. He studied the area and took note of the fact there was no grass or brush along the hollow, only a bed of discolored sediment and flush walls adjacent to the shallow enclosure.

"I think it might be a good idea to pitch your tent higher up. From the looks of it, the water sometimes runs high enough to fill this wash."

Victoria snorted her contempt. "A lot you know about it. That's from the spring thaw when the snow melts. It's the middle of summer.

"Flash floods do happen."

"I've slept here dozens of times, right on that very spot."

"Those clouds might be carrying a lot of water." He again tried to reason with her. "If we get a real downpour of rain up in the higher mountains—"

"For heaven's sake, Cullen, I'm not a child. Please just do as you're told!"

"Ma'am, I—"

"And stop calling me *ma'am*! You're not talking to my mother!"

"I was trying to remain respectful."

"Well, it's totally out of character for you, so don't!"

"Yes, ma'am," he said curtly. "And how should I address you?"

She scowled and clenched her small fists with anger. "You may call me Miss Melbourne."

"That's mighty formal for way out here in the middle of nowhere."

"If you're going to be a pain about it, I suppose you can call me by my first name."

"And you think *ma'am* sounds stuffy!" he heckled her. "*Victoria* might be all right for a social gathering or around your mother and her highbrow friends, but it doesn't fit a spunky little wood nymph running loose out here in the wilderness."

"Perhaps you have a suggestion. What would be your choice? Mistress Wicked Witch? Or maybe Filly? How about Wild Mustang?"

"None of those are quite right," he responded. "Weren't you ever a kid? Didn't you have a nickname? Me, most call me Cully rather than Cullen."

"I've never liked the name Vickie, and Vic is too masculine for a girl."

"You must have another name you like. What do your friends call you?"

"They call me Victoria."

"Won't wash." He flatly refused. "How about we think of something more befitting?"

"Perhaps *spoiled brat*?"

"You're getting warm," he said with a grin, "but it would be disrespectful for my boss' daughter."

"So what name would you choose for me?"

He thought a moment. "How about Sassy, or Sparks?"

"How very complimentary," she said dryly.

"We could try something on a more personal level . . . kitten, beauty, darlin', sweetheart?"

"You're really looking forward to being rid of me, aren't you?" Victoria asked, growing weary of the silly conversation.

"If it's a choice between putting up with you or your mother, I definitely prefer you."

"You think I'm less trouble to be around than her?"

"Not necessarily, but you are much prettier to look at."

Rather than her being flattered, it was as if the fire had been doused in her eyes. When she spoke, there was a mixture of regret and animosity in her voice. "Being pretty has always been a curse to me. I've been decorated and displayed before crowds or at gatherings since I was three years old. Do you know what it's like to be paraded about like a fancy-dressed doll?"

"Uh, well, being a man, it's something I never gave much thought to."

"I can tell you, it's not much fun. *Careful with your dress, dear.*" She used a mocking voice, like her mother. "*Don't muss your hair. No playing with the other children—you might get dirty. Now walk straight, dear. Pull in your tummy, and keep your head up and shoulders back.*" She uttered an oath under her breath. "*And remember to smile!*"

"All of the hard work seems to have paid off. You're about to marry the prize bull of Wyoming."

"Yes, a crowning moment of glory for my mother."

"Is that why she's pushing this marriage on you? She

wants you to wed the richest man in this part of the country?"

"Who said I was being pushed into the marriage?"

"I've seen Winston, remember?" Cully was blunt. "He might make a good town statue, but he isn't going to be much of a husband."

"What do you know about being a husband?"

He ignored the question. "A woman for Winston is going to be like an expensive top hat—something to wear for show."

"He's handsome, charming, and his father is a wealthy man. You know they own the bank, and their ranch is almost as large as our own."

"So all a man needs is money and power to be a worthwhile prize?"

"Winston is running for mayor in November," she countered. "There's a good chance he can win."

"That's why he needs you. The election will be a shoo-in with you at his side."

"You don't have a very high opinion of him."

"Sometimes the biggest fish in the pond turns out to be a sucker or carp, lady. They only look like a trophy while they're in the water. Once caught, you're stuck with a trash fish you can't even eat."

She ignored his sarcastic philosophy and grew pensive. "It doesn't matter what you think of Winston. The wedding will go forward."

"I don't recall the guy ever coming out to visit with you. Did I miss the whole courtship thing?"

"It was not exactly a courtship. Mother spoke with Malcolm Vanderpool at a social function, and the next day I was betrothed to Winston."

"You could have refused."

"Our wedding is more than a marriage; it's also a business deal," she replied. "Our two ranches, once joined, will be the biggest in Wyoming."

"When it comes to marriage, I think I prefer love to a business arrangement."

She smiled. "I believe that's the first time you've ever given me an honest answer."

"Everyone ought to be allowed one mistake," he retorted.

"The last handyman we had was a Mexican who thought he was every woman's dream lover. He would grovel at my mother's feet, do anything to endear himself to her, then ride into town and chase women at night. He was forever sneaking off during the day to catch up on his sleep. We fired him when we caught him kissing the maid." She showed a mischievous smile. "We kept the maid. *They* are too hard to replace."

"But not a worthless, nonachieving, handyman?"

"A dime a dozen," she cooed teasingly. "You're here, aren't you?"

"That does it," he asserted. "I'm going to call you Sparks. The name fits you."

Victoria wrinkled her brow in thought. "All right, Sparks it is . . . if you will answer a personal question."

"Shoot."

"As you are moderately capable with a hammer and forge, plus a trifle smarter than a fence post, is this really the best job you could get?"

"Ex-convicts can't be choosy."

Her eyes widened with shock. "You've been in prison?"

"Thought that might pique your interest," he said impishly.

"What a droll sense of humor you have. My mother would never allow a convict on the place. I'm sure she checked your history."

"Actually, it was your father who hired me."

Victoria knitted her brow in reflection. "Ah, yes, the blackmail scheme I have yet to uncover. Tell me, how do you happen to know my father?"

"We've been close friends for years, he and I," Cully quipped. "We used to go hunting for deer and elk together."

"Father hasn't hunted in years."

"You're right; it was billiards. We used to hang around at the saloon and play by the hour." At another contrary frown, he tried, "Darts at the Irish pub in town?" At the knitting of her neatly-plucked brows, he offered, "Marbles at the school playground?"

"Tell the truth, Cullen. How do you happen to know my father?"

"He was out robbing drunks one night, and we bumped into each other." With a perverse grin, he said, "I was the drunk."

"Can't you be serious?" she cried, exasperated at his evasions. "Do you have to tell lies and stories every time you open your mouth?"

"It's like I told you earlier, the truth is often pretty boring stuff."

"I suppose it doesn't matter." She dismissed his face-tiousness. "Father wouldn't do anything to upset Mother. I don't know where the two of you met, but I'm sure you haven't got a criminal record."

"Not in the name of Cullen Lomax anyway."

She sighed, knowing he was leading her down a fairy-tale path again. "Are you saying your name is not really Cullen Lomax?"

"No, I'm saying we shouldn't pitch your tent so close to the water. If it rains hard enough in the high country, we might get a flood coming down through the gorge. If you were to be washed away and your body never found, I'm pretty sure your mother would blame me. Hate to lose a great job over something as trifling as your drowning."

"I already told you, I've camped here a dozen times before. There's absolutely no danger."

"If you say so."

"I do! Now put my tent right here"—she made it an ultimatum—"or I'll do it myself!"

Cully shrugged his shoulders. "Whatever you say, Sparks."

"I suppose the nickname is better than that *ma'am* stuff."

"Fits too," he said, again showing her his most winning smile. "You're always glowing hot or angry about something."

"It's the company I keep—your company!"

He cast another glance skyward. Dark clouds blotted out the sun. They still roiled high in the atmosphere, which meant they might hold off for a little while longer. But in the distance, a gray curtain was draped against the mountaintops, evidence of rain falling. It appeared there was a storm headed their way.

Chapter Three

Roy Weathers entered the bank and made his way to the office at the back. He didn't have to knock, as the door was partially open. However, he stopped at hearing voices.

". . . wasn't home, Father. She's gone to visit her brother. I made the trip for nothing."

"It's not a problem. I'll see Mrs. Melbourne at the party and make sure everything is on track. She wants this marriage as much as we do."

"Yes, the culmination of your plan since we settled here, Father. I still think—"

"No, you don't!" Malcolm's voice boomed. "You don't *think!* You'll do as I say, and that's the end of it. I know you've been sneaking around with another woman. That's over and done with, you understand?"

"I'm allowed to have a little fun," Winston answered back. "Unlike you, I thought it best to chase around *before* I got married."

"Your mother and I both got what we wanted out of

our marriage." Malcolm's voice was sharp. "You've got a future here—so long as you do as I say. Understand?"

"Yeah, I hear you."

Rather than risk having anyone think he was eavesdropping on the two men, Roy pushed the door open wide and walked into the room.

"Howdy, Winston, Mr. Vanderpool," he greeted the two men. "I know it's about closing time, but I wonder if I could have a moment of your time."

"Certainly, Sheriff," Malcolm replied. "What can we do for you?"

"Don Sanson was shot and killed today. I just finished up with the doc. He says Don was shot at fairly close range—there was a trace of gunpowder on the front of his shirt."

"Don't tell me Don got into a gunfight," Malcolm said.

"Nope, it was murder."

Winston whistled under his breath. "It can't be!" he declared. "Who would want to kill Mr. Sanson? He was as nice a guy as there is in the entire country."

"I'm looking into it, but it doesn't look as if there were any witnesses."

"What do you want from us, Sheriff?" Malcolm asked.

"I'm told Don had a mortgage on his place. Can you give me any other information?"

Malcolm got up from his desk and walked to a nearby bookcase, where a number of ledgers stood neatly in a row. He removed one and placed it on his desk.

"I've got the entry right here," he told Roy, opening the journal. "Don was going to make the payment on his mortgage after he sold some beef. I wasn't worried about lending him money. He was honest as the day is long."

Malcolm flipped a few pages and stopped, placing a finger on an underlined figure. "Here it is—a balance of thirty-three hundred dollars and some odd change. Don hoped to pay off about half of the principle after the fall roundup."

"That cattle sickness really hurt him and Melbourne last year," Roy said. "I remember his saying how he hated going into debt."

"Yes, he told me the same thing when he signed the loan papers."

"I don't suppose he listed an heir to his property, did he?"

"Only his wife," Malcolm replied. "No way he could have known he would die within a few months of her passing."

"What will happen to his place?"

"The bank will continue to run it until a search can be made for any next-of-kin. If we can't locate anyone, the place will be sold for what is owed, along with taxes and upkeep."

"I'm not aware of any potential buyers in town," Roy said. "Any idea when a sale might come about?"

"Far as I know, Don didn't have any living relatives. An uncle and two brothers died when he was a boy.

I mentioned he should have an heir after his wife passed, but he never got around to naming anyone."

"I don't suppose anyone has inquired about his ranch in the past while?" Roy asked. "Any suspicious types?"

"Sorry, Sheriff," Malcolm said, "but no. I can't imagine why anyone would want to kill someone like Don. He was liked by everyone who knew him."

"How about you, Winston?" Roy questioned the Vanderpool son. "I don't suppose anyone has approached you about Don or his place?"

"My boy has no head for business," Malcolm cut in abruptly, not allowing Winston to answer. "He spends most of his time running our ranch. Why would you want to ask him about Don's ranch or affairs?"

"I'm going to ask everyone until I run out of people to ask," Roy informed the elder Vanderpool civilly. "I don't have a single clue as to who the killer is, so I'm hoping someone around town will have an opinion."

"Yes, of course." Malcolm was brusque. "Opinions are like mouths—everybody has one, but few have anything worthwhile to say. I wager you'll draw a blank."

"I can't think of anything that might be of help," Winston offered. "But I'll ask the boys out at the ranch. Maybe somebody came by asking questions while I was in town."

"Thanks, Winston, I'd appreciate the help."

"I'll get in touch if I learn anything, Sheriff. Anything at all."

Roy said his thanks and left the two men. He hadn't

eaten since breakfast, so he would stop at the café for a bite, talk to a few people, and turn in early. He would start fresh come morning, likely without a single clue or any idea of where to look for a cold-blooded killer.

Victoria walked along the creek, found a patch of grass near the summit of a hill, and sat for a time. Due to the lateness of the afternoon, she didn't walk too far from the buggy. A rumble in the distance warned of on-coming rain. She crossed her arms, realizing she should have worn a jacket. With the dark clouds overhead, the temperature was growing cool, and a chilling breeze tickled its way through the nearby foliage.

She battled a feeling of depression, wishing her life was her own. The marriage loomed over her as darkly as the impending storm. She hardly knew Winston. They had spoken once or twice, but they had never sat down and had a real conversation. How could she marry some-one she didn't even know?

She hated the fears and angst that assailed her every waking moment. All of her girlish dreams about love and romance had been dashed. She was to sacrifice her own life for the good of her family. It was a burden she had to bear. Blinking back tears of helpless frustration, she sat for a short while longer and then returned to camp.

Victoria discovered Cully busy at the campfire, fry-ing something in a pan and working to prepare their supper. Watching from a discreet distance, she set aside her dark mood and wondered about the strange handyman. Cullen Lomax was capable, intelligent, and behind his expressive hazel eyes seemed to lie a complex mystery. He had shown his patience and humor on numerous occasions, yet something about him warned he could be serious and deadly if the need were to arise.

Five or six inches taller than her own five-foot-four, he was fit, moved with dexterity and ease, and handled any task given to him. The two of them had been thrown together a number of times, but she had been careful not to show him any favor. After all, he was only a hired hand. Her mother would have fired him in an instant if she discovered the two of them had actually become friends.

The wind swept over the hills, a cold blast of air to remind her of the approaching storm. A glance over her shoulder told her the dark curtain, while still a long way off in the distance, was moving in their direction. She walked over to take advantage of the warmth from the fire.

"Starting to get cold," she asserted, settling down on her haunches and extending her hands toward the flames.

Cully paused to assess the ominous clouds. "We'll be getting wet in an hour or less."

"We'd better eat and get to cover."

"The food is ready," he said. "Grab a plate."

She sat down on a rock, while he forked a portion of fried potatoes and ham strips from the skillet, then spooned warm beans straight from a can. The food smelled great, and Victoria was hungry. After the first couple of bites, she looked at Cully with a new respect.

"Hmm, maybe Daddy's idea about your coming along wasn't such a bad one. You're a pretty good cook."

"It helps that you're half-starved from skipping lunch."

She laughed. "Where did you learn to fry potatoes like this? They're tender but sort of crispy too."

"I could tell you it's an old Indian recipe," he said.

"Is it?"

"No, I don't know any old Indians."

"You spout a great many tales. It's hard to believe anything you say."

"It's my way of adding something to the conversation. I wouldn't lie to you about anything really important."

"You only lie for amusement—is that what you're saying?"

"Yup, my stories are intended to entertain, not deceive," Cully clarified.

It began to sprinkle, so they hurried to finish eating. Victoria didn't leave Cully to do all of the work, helping to clean the dishes and get things stowed away before the rain started to seriously come down.

Cully worked quickly to put the supplies away, tucking almost everything into the runabout. It was the oldest of the Melbournes' four wagons but the only buggy built to be pulled by a single horse. The worn, patched-canvas top was open on three sides, but it was parked opposite the wind, so everything would be as protected as possible. He waited until Victoria had retreated to her tent before he kicked out the fire. With a last look at the creek and the tethered horse, he hurried up the slope and over the crest of the hill to his own dwelling.

Considering they were in for a real downpour, he was glad he had taken the time to scrape a runoff ditch along the base of both shelters. It would allow any buildup of water to be drained away from the tents, thus preventing it from forming a puddle and seeping inside. Ducking out of the rain, he removed and placed his boots at the inside entrance and lay back on top of the blankets. With the presence of the storm, he would continue to monitor the level of the stream and make sure Victoria was comfortable for the night.

Bud Longmont was waiting at the side door of the boardinghouse. Sandra's brother seemed to always be around. He was not exactly intimidating, but he was watchful over his sister. Winston gave him a nod of greeting and entered through the door. The side entrance allowed him to access the stairway without being seen by anyone in the main sitting room. His footsteps were lightly placed so as not to make any more noise than necessary. He quickly reached the second floor and went to the end of the hall. A light tap was all it took, and the door was thrown open.

"I wasn't sure you were coming," Sandra said. "I was about to go to bed."

Winston looked over her dressing gown and smiled. With her hair brushed out and lying loose to her shoulders, she looked very much like a siren from a painting he had once seen. He said as much, and she flushed.

"You shouldn't be here at all . . . not with me in my nightclothes."

"The day will come when there will be no need for shyness, my love."

His words should have brightened her face with anticipation, but she grew somber. "Not if your father has his way. I overheard a couple of women in the store saying Victoria Melbourne is going to become your wife. Bud says I shouldn't see you anymore."

Winston reached out and took hold of Sandra. She offered a virginal resistance, but he coerced her to his chest. Gazing down into her face, he mustered forth his most sincere expression.

"No, no, Sandra, my dear," Winston said. "Fate has come forth to change everything. Don Sanson was killed earlier today. My father holds the mortgage to his ranch."

"I remember your telling me that your father had acquired mortgages on the Sanson and Melbourne ranches after they both had bad seasons last year. But how does Mr. Sanson's death change anything between us?"

"Don't you see?" Winston was eager now. "Father assured me that we are going to gain control of the Sanson place, because we hold the mortgage. Once we have his ranch, we'll have access to the river for our cattle. We won't need the Melbourne place!"

Sandra's face lit up at the news. "If you don't need their ranch, you won't have to marry Victoria!"

"Exactly!"

Sandra rewarded the news with a warm kiss, and Winston's mood soared. He held her tightly, and they kissed a second time.

"It's all going to work out," he promised. "You'll see."

The girl pushed him back and studied his face. "You didn't have anything to do with Sanson's death, did you?"

He laughed at the notion. "Not that I wouldn't gladly kill for you, my love, but no, I don't know anything about his murder."

"And your father?"

Winston sobered. "When it comes to wealth and power, there isn't much I would put past him. However, I don't have any reason to think he would hire someone to kill Don Sanson." He lifted a shoulder in a shrug. "After all, he had already arranged the marriage to give him the same access to the river."

"I want to believe this makes a difference," Sandra said. "But I don't trust your father. What if he decides he wants the entire valley? I have a hard time believing he will let you out of the wedding without a fight."

Winston frowned. He knew the unquenchable thirst his father had for power. The idea of controlling three ranches instead of two would appeal to him. He might well think of this as an opportunity for more. A man driven by greed has no conscience or compassion, and his father was such a man.

"I'm going to speak to him."

"He won't listen," she said. "You've told me a hundred times how he never listens to a word you say."

"What do you want me to do?" Winston asked. "You're the only thing I want out of life."

"Tell your father you are calling off the wedding, that you won't marry Victoria under any circumstances. He can't force you to wed someone if you absolutely refuse to go along."

Before he could prevent it, fear sneaked into his expression. "Would you have me disowned?" he asked. "I never learned a trade. I help in the bank and manage the paperwork on the ranch—what kind of job could I get?"

"Your father has to take your happiness into consideration!" Sandra declared. "Stand up to him. Convince him that your feelings must count for something."

"I will, I promise," he vowed. "I'll make him understand."

Sandra came back into his arms. Her lips were sweet and warm, promising a love that would lift him to the heavens. He had to find a way to persuade his father to stop the wedding.

Victoria was lost within a dreamless slumber when something abruptly caused her to awaken. She blinked against the darkness, able to discern an odd rumbling and peculiar kind of crunching noise. Victoria strained to listen. The downpour of rain was loud against the tent roof, but this sounded like . . . She rose up onto her elbows. It was as if a pile of sticks was being pushed along by a broom. She immediately thought of Cully. He must be walking about and had crushed a branch under-foot. But even as she sat upright, her small shelter was hit by a wall of water.

Victoria scrambled to kick free of the blankets, but icy-cold water rushed in and utterly swamped the tent. Her world turned into a whirlpool of glacial liquid. She was upended and rolled over from the frightful force. Entangled in her bedding, she was propelled along with the enormous onrush of floodwater and debris. The swells engulfed her and plunged her head-over-heels into the depths of the raging water. Victoria splashed to surface, gasped for air, and screamed as loudly as she could.

"Cully!"

Chapter Four

Cully, worried about the cloudburst, had been moving down the hill to check on the horse when he heard the rumble of floodwater coming into the wash. The ground underfoot was slippery from the rain, but he hastened his pace. He topped the rim above Victoria's tent in time to hear her shriek his name in terror. Through the gloom and deluge of rain, he saw the shelter ripped from the ground and disappear in a murky, swiftly moving, black mass of water.

He risked a fall from the uncertain footing as he raced along the side of the hill to get ahead of the tumbling, half-submerged tent. His memory flashed back to the way the glen narrowed to funnel through a gap only a short way down the hill. He had to get Victoria out of her tent, or she would drown, but to plunge into the frothing water and try to swim would mean death for them both. His only chance was to reach the narrow opening and snare her where the water was forced to funnel through the confined channel.

He blinked against the rain in his eyes and sprinted along the slippery high ground to the gap. It was dark, but a lightning bolt brightened the night and offered him a momentary twinkling of light. He spied the nearly submerged top of the tent and plunged into the frigid water. The current hit him with such force, it nearly swept his feet out from under him. He sought a solid rock footing and half waded and half swam until he was chest high in the fierce torrent.

A portion of the shelter surfaced a few feet from him, propelled violently toward the break between the two rock walls. Cully grabbed hold of the wet canvas and struggled mightily to pull it back to shore. The fierce rush of water and debris slammed against him, but he righted himself and maintained his grip. He splashed about with his free hand to preserve his balance and used all of his strength to yank the shelter toward the rocky wall, where he pinned it against a slippery boulder.

The raging river swirled and crashed brutally against him, threatening to rip the material from his grasp at any second. He shoved his arm between the folds of canvas, trying to get hold of the girl.

"Victoria!" he shouted over the noisy roar of water, "take my hand!"

He feared she was unconscious, drowning at that very moment, but then Victoria's long-nailed fingers clamped a viselike grip onto his arm. She climbed him like a tree branch, pulling herself out of the twisted section of tent, thrashing frantically to free herself from the tangle of blankets. Cully braced himself, fortified against the vigorous current, while Victoria splashed and floundered madly, clinging to him with all her might. She climbed upward, wrapped her arms about his neck, and kicked free of the bedding.

She coughed and choked, unable to draw in sufficient air, strangling from the amount of water she'd swallowed. Cully rotated, sought a sure foundation for his footing, and waded for shore. He staggered against the fierce on-rush of water and reached the bank. Then he hefted the girl bodily up onto the muddy turf and, with a shove, pushed her well up the bank. He quickly followed her out of the water.

Victoria rolled onto her stomach, gagging and retch-ing, spitting out liquid and trying to suck oxygen into her lungs. Cully moved to straddle her, wrapped his arms around her abdomen and lifted, upending her several inches, helping her to regurgitate the water. After a few terrible seconds, she began to suck in great gulps of air.

"I-I'm all right!" she panted at last, and she waved a hand as a signal for him to release her.

Cully let go and sagged down next to her, exhausted from the frightful experience and intense effort. He felt an icy chill, more so at the thought of losing Victoria than from being soaked and cold.

A few more seconds . . . If he had been asleep, if the canvas shelter had not remained near the surface, if he had not decided to check on her . . . *If, if, if!* The trip had almost been a fatal disaster.

"I-I was . . ." A flash of lightning revealed that Victo-ria's complexion was ashen and her eyes were broadened from fright. "I was . . . I couldn't see!" she gasped. "I couldn't breathe—the water—I was trapped in the blankets. They wrapped about my legs like tentacles from a great sea beast and pulled me down."

Cully reached out to put an arm around her shoulders to comfort her. Victoria needed more than that. She practically vaulted into his arms, ducking her head against his chest, throwing her arms around his waist and hugging him tightly. "I thought . . . I thought I was going to die," she sobbed.

"It's okay," Cully whispered, his chin above her ear, encircling her protectively in his embrace. "It's over. You're safe now."

Victoria clung to him, squeezing him so tightly, he had a hard time getting any air into his own lungs. It had been a very close call. Another second or two underwater and she would have lost consciousness. A missed step on the slippery rock, a loss of grip on the half-submerged shelter, being struck by a floating log—a hundred things could have prevented him from getting her out. The prospect of such a dire outcome caused Cully to tighten his hold on the girl.

"It's all right, Sparks," he whispered after a short span of time. "I wouldn't let anything happen to you."

The sound of his voice helped Victoria regain her composure. "I-I'm all right," she murmured against his shoulder. "If you hadn't . . ."

"Had me worried for a minute or two." He tried to lighten the mood. "If you had drowned, your mother would have positively made my life miserable." He let the words hang for a moment and added, "Even more miserable, I should say."

"Father would have been a little upset too," she said in return. "After all, he sent you to watch over me."

"Yep. I would have hated to let Jeff down."

Victoria had recovered her poise and released her death grip. She sought to sit upright as Cully liberated her from his hold.

"What do you think, a late-spring thaw?" he asked, referring to her notion that flood conditions were impossible. "Must have been some snowpack left back in the higher mountains."

"Obviously," she replied, salvaging her pluck. "It's the only possible explanation."

He chuckled, and Victoria displayed a smile. She stared at Cully in the darkness, her hair pasted to her scalp and shoulders. She took a moment to brush water from her face and eyes with the backs of her hands. Another streak of lightning illuminated the world fleetingly. It permitted Cully to see the girl, clad in her soaked underdress and still trembling.

"Let's get up to my tent. I've got a towel you can use to dry off."

"I'll need some dry clothes," Victoria said, standing upright. She took a step and yelped in pain. "Ouch! The rocks along here are about as sharp as broken glass."

Without asking permission, Cully put an arm around her shoulders and the other under the back of her knees and lifted her off of her feet. She inhaled a sharp breath, surprised by his action.

"What are you doing?"

"I thought I'd check to see how much you weighed," he said, kidding. "We need to make certain a much weaker man—say, a social type like your betrothed—can carry you across the threshold on your wedding night."

"Just don't drop me!"

"I'm more worried I'll slip and *not* drop you," he quipped. "You'd sure enough come down on top of me."

Cully took his time, picking his way along the treacherous slope, puffing from the effort. After a few moments Victoria mused, "So, the handyman is a gallant gentleman after all. I hadn't considered you to be the chivalrous sort."

"If I slip and we slide down the bank and land in that raging floodwater, chivalry will die a quick death—it'll be every man or woman for themselves."

Victoria laced her arms around his neck, helping to distribute her weight on such uncertain footing. Cully made his way to a gradual incline where he was able to climb up the bank and reach the trail. The rain had abated to a drizzle, with only an occasional flash of lightning. When he reached the tent, he set Victoria down at the entrance. She immediately crossed her arms to hug herself.

"Hurry up with a towel or something, Cully," she stammered, shivering from head to toe, "I-I'm about to f-freeze out here."

Cully opened the tent flap and retrieved a drying cloth. He offered it to Victoria and said, "We don't want to get the bedding all wet. Dry off as best you can, and get out of your wet clothes."

"And what am I supposed to wear?"

"I'll be back with your luggage by the time you get dried off."

She glanced at the tent. "What about the sleeping arrangements?"

Cully grinned. "I'm enough of a gentleman that I won't ask you to sleep out in the rain."

"How very gracious of you."

"Just dry yourself off, and get inside. We'll discuss the sleeping arrangements after I'm out of the rain too."

He thought she would argue further, but she trembled violently, and her teeth continued to chatter uncontrollably. "All right, I'm t-too cold to argue," she capitulated.

Cully left her with the towel and walked over the hill to the runabout. He returned a few moments later, and she was inside the tent. Victoria had used the towel to wipe the mud off of her feet and left it hanging on the edge of the tent roof.

He paused to pass the suitcase into the shelter. While she got into a fresh set of clothes, he removed his boots and knocked off as much mud as he could. He spoke a warning, entered the tent, and crawled onto the blankets.

"We . . . we can't sleep together." Victoria's voice squeaked. "I mean, it . . . it isn't decent."

"Pilgrims have to make do," Cully replied. "I'll trust you not to take advantage of the situation." He waited— she didn't reply—so he added, "We don't have a lot of options."

"Yes, yes, I understand," she muttered. "But this is completely mortifying!"

He smiled to himself. "We will both be fully dressed, except for our shoes, and I'll do my best not to disturb you during the night."

"That means no touching of my person—not even by accident!"

"Whatever you say, Sparks."

It was as dark as the inside of a tomb, but Cully managed to change into his spare trousers and shirt. He felt around until he was able to find his way under the blankets. Careful to avoid contact with Victoria, he lay back and tried to relax.

"C-Cully," Victoria shivered through her chattering teeth, "I-I'm really cold. I can't . . . can't s-stop shaking."

"It's a wonder you didn't suffer shock," he said earnestly. "That was damn scary—for both of us."

"That's the f-first time I ever heard you use even a mild p-profanity before," she said, stammering from being cold.

"A person shouldn't swear unless it's called for," he explained. "Your about dying is way up on the top of my list."

Victoria was silent for a moment, but she was obviously suffering chills. "Cully, do you have any more blankets?"

"Not even a jacket," he said. "Someone didn't give me a lot of time to pack."

She hesitated. "Would you . . . could we . . . can we cuddle a little?" she managed weakly, her voice sounding as timid as a child. "Just till I get warm?"

He didn't force her to ask a second time. He turned slightly onto his side, awkward as it was, and slipped his arms around her. She slid in close, keeping her arms tucked in at her sides with her hands across her chest, allowing him to hold her close yet disallowing the intimacy of dancing or sharing a hug. After a few intensely awkward moments, she relaxed within his grasp.

"How come you're so warm?" she asked after a short time. "We both got soaked, and we're sharing the same blankets."

"Blame it on human nature," he said.

"Human nature?"

"Yeah. You only have a low-life, nonachieving handyman to cozy up to. Me? I've got my arms around the prettiest gal in Wyoming."

He couldn't see her face, but he felt she was smiling.

"Are you ever serious?"

"Not anymore," he said with a degree of candor. "Being serious about got me killed a time or two."

Those were the final words between them. After a few minutes, Victoria ceased shivering and withdrew from Cully's grasp. Wordlessly, she moved back to her own side of the blankets and turned onto her back. It didn't take long before it sounded as if she had gone to sleep.

Cully was tired too and could feel the first hint of sore muscles from the rescue and carrying Victoria up to the tent. He vowed to take the sensible approach to the situation. He would be smart, resolved, and simply push her out of his mind so he could get some sleep.

Right. As if I'm going to forget that such a beautiful and desirable woman is lying only inches away.

Concho sat in the darkest corner of the saloon. He took the money owed him and stuck it into his pocket.

"He wouldn't listen to reason?" his current employer asked.

"I tried to make him a handsome offer, but he wasn't of the mind to listen. He said he had no intention of selling even one square foot of his place."

"The damned fool! He didn't need all that range."

"Yeah, too bad he was so hardheaded about it. Now he's only going to own about a six-foot by four-foot section of it for his resting place."

"You going to be around town for a few days?"

"I can stay close by for a time," Concho replied. "You got another job lined up for me?"

"It's possible."

"If it's a second killing, it might stir up a passel of trouble. Your local sheriff might even call in the U.S. Marshal."

"I hired you because of your reputation for doing whatever the job called for."

The man grinned. "True enough, my friend, if the money is right."

"I should know by tomorrow night."

"I'll be in touch." Concho was agreeable. "Just remember, a second chore might cost more, because of the risk."

"We'll discuss payment once I know if I need you or not."

"You can trust me; I'll see the job gets done right."

The man said he understood and then pushed back from the table and rose to his feet. With a tip of his head as farewell, he turned around and left the room.

Concho stroked his trimmed moustache and watched his employer leave. Not a man to question fate, he wondered what had driven his employer to order the death of an innocent man. It seemed a drastic step for only a small piece of land. He grunted his disdain for the human race.

One day we'll be killing each other for a pair of boots or over the cut of a man's clothes. The thought caused him to smile. *At least there will always be work for someone like me!*

The funeral was attended by some fifty people. Roy Weathers looked over the faces of the crowd and recognized most of them. He paused when he spied Sandra Longmont and her brother, Bud, among the gathering. She was not strikingly beautiful, but she was attractive and had thick, beautiful hair—usually worn up but loose about her shoulders this day. He knew she worked at the dress shop with Widow Ingle. Her brother did odd jobs around town, was soft-spoken, and had never caused any trouble. Roy had not talked to either of them concerning the murder, as they were relatively new in town. He did know Sandra was the woman Winston Vanderpool had been seeing on the sly. If not for the grim reality of the moment, he would have smiled. Practically everyone knew about the two of them. It must have put a crimp into their relationship when Winston's father made a formal announcement of his son's engagement to Victoria Melbourne.

He listened to the final words being spoken about Don Sanson, and a heavy burden of responsibility imbued his shoulders. A man was dead, a good man, and everyone was looking to him to find his killer. A final "amen" ended the ceremony. As the crowd began to break up, Jeff Melbourne hobbled over to speak to him. He knew what was coming yet had nothing positive to report.

"Anything on the murdering varmint who did this?" Jeff asked the expected question.

"I can't even figure a motive, Jeff. Don had no enemies."

"Strikes a man odd that he lost half his herd to sickness last year, and before he has a chance to get back on his feet, he's murdered."

"Your herd was hit by the sickness too," Roy said. "Do you think someone has it in for both of you?"

"Could be," Jeff replied. "Funny how the disease never affected Vanderpool's herd."

Roy displayed a grim humor. "He's too wealthy and powerful for any ordinary bug or whatever to tackle. Didn't you discover it to be Texas fever?"

"That's what some old-timer who works for Malcolm said. He stopped by and had a look at the cattle. He said he'd seen the same sickness before, and it was sure enough Texas fever." Jeff changed positions to rest his lame leg.

"Do you remember back when the first longhorns were driven through eastern Kansas and Missouri, how the local ranchers had to ban the herds to keep those cattle from infecting their own beef? The claim was that the deadly fever killed local cattle, but it never harmed the longhorn."

"Yeah, I remember," Roy agreed. "That's when the drovers had to start shipping Texas cattle from places like Abilene and Dodge City." He frowned in thought. "You don't figure someone sneaked a few head of infected cattle through from down Texas way—maybe rustlers or cowboys with a small herd—and they passed the disease to Don's and your beef?"

Jeff sighed. "Can't say where it came from, Roy, but it didn't return this year. Good thing too, after it cost me and Don nearly a thousand head of cattle between us."

"I saw the smoke from the fires all the way back in town," Roy told Jeff. "Got to be heartbreaking to slaughter half of your herd because of some damnable disease."

"Hardest thing I ever did, aside from burying a close friend or relative—that's the truth."

"Don had to take out a mortgage to keep the ranch going." Roy turned back to business. "How did you weather the loss?"

"I already had a note against my place, so I had to borrow even more. The ranch is the deepest in debt it has ever been."

"This is not what a man needs when he reaches our age, huh?" Roy said. "You've got a big mortgage on your place, and I have to try to find a stone-cold killer. Hell, the two of us ought to be spending our days fishing."

"Are you going to try to get some outside help?" Jeff immediately raised a hand, as if to prevent a heated reply. "It's not that I don't think you're a capable lawman, Roy, but this is a murder. It's a little different than settling a domestic argument or stopping a barroom fight. I know you've never had any specialized training for something like this."

"I sent off a wire to the U.S. Marshal's office, but they have fewer than a dozen men to handle a thousand square miles. I don't expect them to send anyone to investigate a single shooting."

Jeff glanced around, as if making sure no one was eavesdropping on their conversation. When he spoke, his voice was hushed. "I happen to know of someone of experience who could lend a hand. If you'd like, I'll speak to him."

"Pride is something I set aside when it comes to solving a murder, Melbourne," Roy told him seriously. "I'm a blind man in a cornfield, trying to find the shortest route to the wagon. If you know someone who can help, I'll put him on the scent and turn him loose."

Roy graciously accepted Jeff's explanation as to why he thought this particular man could help. Then Roy watched him limp back over to stand with his wife. When Martha caught him looking their direction, she smiled at him. Roy could not prevent a smile from leaping to his own lips. He had known Martha since childhood. She grew up haughty and vain and could be a real brat, but he had seen her occasionally display a caring and tender side. He had stood back and watched her over the years, always out of reach yet within sight. Being ten years older than she, he was off seeking his fortune when she matured from a teen into a lady. By the time he returned, she had married Jefford Melbourne, a decent and likable fellow.

The two of them turned, arm in arm, and walked toward their buckboard. It struck him as curious that they had not come in their runabout, which was a much more comfortable ride, but Martha's presence caused him to lose any normal train of thought. He wondered even now about how different his life might have been had he taken the chance and made the attempt to court her.

"Anything new on the shooter?" Malcolm Vanderpool's voice interrupted Roy's daydreaming. He rotated to face the banker.

"Nothing yet."

"I just spoke to Don's three hired men," Malcolm informed him. "I'm sending Zeke Pullman over from my ranch to ramrod the Sanson spread until this is settled."

Roy recalled that Zeke Pullman was the old-timer who had diagnosed the Texas fever in Don and Jeff's beef. "I would guess, with all of his years experience, he's as cattle-wise as a seasoned bull," he said to Malcolm.

"My son will handle the bookkeeping end of things, so Zeke only has to manage the hired hands and see that everything is taken care of."

"If you acquire the Sanson place and combine it with

your own, you'll have a bigger spread than the Melbourne ranch."

Malcolm dismissed the statement. "Come next month, when my son marries Jeff's daughter, the point will be moot. With our two spreads combined, we will have the largest ranch this side of New Mexico, with or without Sanson's spread."

"I guess that means you're going ahead with the wedding," Roy deduced. "A charming and beautiful girl, Victoria Melbourne."

"Nothing but the finest for my son," Malcolm said smugly.

Roy didn't comment on that. He knew that Winston liked to carouse at the local saloons, and there was also his clandestine relationship with Sandra Longmont. Moreover, he liked to gamble and would sometimes play until the wee hours of the morning. As dedicated as Malcolm was in attaining power and wealth, Winston didn't seem to care about it one way or the other.

"I'll talk to you later, Sheriff," Malcolm said, striding off to join his son.

Roy took a last look around at the few stragglers. One of them might have been responsible for the murder of Don Sanson, but he had no idea as to the why. All he could do was keep asking questions and hope someone offered a bit of information that would help point him in a direction.

Chapter Five

The Melbourne Inn was an eatery and rooming house. More than a weigh station for stagecoach travel, it was located at a crossroads to any of four different directions. Hunters, pilgrim travelers, salesmen, businessmen, families moving from one place to another—Avery had chosen the site well. With the nearest railway line fifty miles away, the inn had quickly become a hub for supplies, meals, and staying over for a night or two.

Cully had taken on the chore of driving Mrs. Butters. He slowed the horse as the inn came into sight. He had never seen the place before and was impressed; it was two stories high, with six chimney stacks visible, and over a dozen windows facing their approach. Off a short way was an enormous barn, two bunkhouses, and some storage sheds. Within the expansive corral were no fewer than thirty sturdy-looking stagecoach or freight horses and a dozen mules.

"Twenty-four guest rooms," Victoria boasted, "fifteen

hired men, with two cooks, and tables enough for forty diners at one time."

"It's a lot bigger than I had expected."

"My brother has contracts with several stage and freight lines. People coming in from Utah or Montana can stay a night or two and then take the stage to the railway or back to the Dakotas or even back east."

"I've stayed at an inn or two when I was traveling," Cully told her, "but I've never seen a grander-looking place."

"Mother told Avery he would be broke and living back at home in six months." She did not hide her pride. "He showed her—showed everyone."

"I assume you two were close when he was living at home?"

"Very. He's six years older than I, but he used to take me with him when he went to town or ran an errand. I could always talk to him, and he gave me advice and listened to my troubles." She cast a sidelong glance at Cully. He caught the look but didn't know what it meant. "You remind me of him sometimes . . . when you're not being a tease or a bore."

"I suspect that is the nicest thing you've ever said to me, Sparks."

A rush of color came into her cheeks, and she quickly turned away. "I was referring to your rescue last night. You were very . . . considerate."

"Being a handyman, it's my job," he said.

"Another part of your job is prudence. I'll trust you not to say anything about my little mishap last night."

"Loyal as a hound dog and mum as an apple blossom—that's me."

She smiled—genuinely, as if she had enjoyed his reply—and pointed to a large building. "You can park the runabout next to the barn and stable the horse at one of the inside stalls. Mrs. Butters deserves extra rations of grain and hay before our return trip."

"I'll let you off at the door and tend to the horse and buggy," Cully volunteered.

Fifteen minutes later, he was carrying her bag into the reception area of the inn. A moderately attractive young woman was sitting at a desk. She offered him a smile and stood up.

"You're with my sister-in-law . . . Mr. Cullen Lomax?"

"Yes, ma'am, and you would be Avery's wife."

"It's good Victoria was able to make it over for a visitation," she replied. "Avery speaks of her often."

"As does she about him," Cully replied. "This is her bag."

She signaled to a boy of about twelve or thirteen. "Take the luggage up to number six, Paco." He didn't hesitate but hurried over, took the suitcase, and turned for the stairs.

"We have a stage due in and a number of people staying over to make other connections." Avery Melbourne's wife spoke to Cully again. "I hope you won't take offense if we bunk you with the hired help. I'm afraid it's the only room we have."

"It'll do just fine, Mrs. Melbourne. 'Most anything beats sleeping on the ground."

"However, we would be happy to have you dine with us."

"I'm only a hired hand," he answered. "I prefer to take my meals with the working boys—more comfortable all around."

The lady gave him a curious look. "I overheard Victoria speaking to Avery about you, and I thought perhaps you were more like friends than employer and employee."

Cully had to remind himself not to let his mouth drop open. He recovered after the momentary lapse and smiled. "I'm sure it only seemed that way since she is excited and happy about being here to visit. I'm just the family handyman and her driver."

"I'm sorry," the woman apologized, "I didn't mean to insinuate there was anything more personal between you and her."

"Not at all," he said quickly. "I'm right pleased to think she considers me capable."

"I'll have Paco show you where you can wash up. He'll also find you an empty bed and show you where the hired help take their meals." She waved at the young boy who had taken Victoria's bag to her room and introduced him to Cully. She explained what she wanted, and Paco led the way back out the front door.

Cully said a quick "Thank you" and left the main building. As he followed the boy to see where he would be sleeping, he had to grin. One thing he knew without question—even sharing a bunkhouse, he was sure to get more sleep than he had the previous night.

Roy Weathers looked over the journals Don Sanson had kept on the ranch. One was used for payroll; another concerned his cattle—ages, number of offspring produced, roundup figures, and yearly drives to market; and the third was his bank and accounting book. Everything was neat and in order, with not a single figure standing out. He paused to look over a couple of old photographs among his things.

He spied one of a youthful-looking Don and a little boy. Flipping the picture over, he read the names and date on the back. Next he spent some time sorting through a box filled with old papers and letters. He found only one thing of interest and stuck it into his pocket.

Zeke Pullman was busy rearranging the house to suit his needs. A man with thirty years of cattle experience, his skin was tan and weathered from years in the sun. Though slight of build, he seemed spry enough for his fifty or so years.

Roy walked into the kitchen, where Zeke was sorting some dishware and pans. The man paused in his chore and showed a smile that revealed a couple of missing teeth.

"Never had run of a house this size before," he said. "Looks like Don's wife enjoyed entertaining folks—got enough dishes here to seat half the town at the table."

"I'm a little surprised Malcolm gave you the job of

managing this place. You've only been working for him a short while, haven't you?"

"Started 'bout the middle of last year," Zeke informed him. "And it surprised me too when Malcolm chose me to come here to kind of oversee the place."

"I 'spect you've got more experience than most of his hired men."

"Yep. I drove cattle up the Chisholm Trail back when I was young enough to think sleeping on the ground made a man tough. Tackled more than a few trail drives with Charles Goodnight too." He chuckled. "Guess that shows my age. Everyone knows what a chuck wagon is today, but he was the one who first designed the grub buggy and gave it a name."

"I've heard stories about him—never anything bad."

"He was a good boss, but the long hours in the saddle began to wear me down. I come up this-a-way to find something a mite easier on my bones."

"How are you getting along with the hired hands here?"

"They are good boys, one and all," Zeke replied. "I don't think I could have handpicked three better riders from the Vanderpool spread."

"Malcolm has—what, six or seven men?"

"Closer to a dozen, if you count the cook." Zeke grinned. "Way I heard it, Vanderpool inherited big money—earned from some garment industry his father owned back east. When his pa died, Malcolm sold everything and came west. I can't say he picked the best place to stop, but he has set down roots and is expanding all the time. He's even been in talks with the railroad about putting a spur up this way. The man thinks bigger than the whole outdoors."

Roy remembered how Malcolm Vanderpool had blown into town like a gust of wind and opened a bank the second week after he arrived. A new building went up, and prosperity came to the valley. With his money and pull, it was likely Elk City would grow into a sizable place one day.

"How is it working out for Winston?" he asked. "I know he works a day or two a week at the bank, but he also spends a lot of time at the saloon—too much to be much of a ranch foreman."

"Not much for him to do out there, Sheriff. We have several top hands who practically run the place by themselves. And it isn't like we have a couple thousand head of cattle to watch over. Limited feed and water have caused Malcolm to hold down the number of beef on the place."

"Guess that will all change once his boy marries Miss Melbourne."

Zeke snorted. "Talk about your shotgun weddings—Winston and the Melbourne gal will be like two buffalo trying to dance on their hind legs. The boy don't want any part of the wedding. He's been brooding like a scolded pup ever since his pa arranged the whole deal."

"Well, Victoria is the most sought-after girl in this part of the country," Roy said. "I can't imagine any man not wanting her."

"Ain't saying he wouldn't maybe want her on his

own," Zeke replied. "But—you said it yourself—he loves the night life and good times. Plus he has an eye for another woman. Most wives frown on such antics, once they've got that ring on their finger."

Roy laughed to dismiss the seriousness of their conversation. "Sounds like there will be some sparks flying after those two are hobbled together."

Zeke laughed as well. "It'll be something to watch . . . but from a safe distance. Less chance of getting hit with something that way."

Roy left the old cowpoke and mounted his horse. He had an idea and wanted to get back to town. The telegrapher was an old friend of his and also put out a weekly newsletter. He would get his pal to do some searching for him and see what he could find. It was possible there was a piece missing from this chessboard. If so, maybe he could use it to flush out a killer.

Winston glanced around, fearful his father would be watching. Seeing no one on the street, he quickly crossed to the alleyway between Mildred's Boutique and the tool and tack shop. He didn't have to wait—Sandra was there in the shadows waiting for him.

"I thought you might have changed your mind," she said, a tremor of uncertainty in her voice. "I've been waiting for nearly an hour."

Winston found her warm and yielding within the darkness. She felt wonderful in his arms, her soft, pliant lips moist and eager. He kissed her and relished every second of the contact.

"Wait!" Sandra gasped, pushing out of his arms. "I can't do this. *We* can't do this!"

"But it feels so right," Winston replied, resisting the urge to drop down to his knees and beg. "Come on, dearest, you know it's what we both want."

"We have to hide in the shadows like curious schoolkids," she complained. "I'm not some shady saloon girl or a married woman cheating on her husband. I'm respectable and have no attachments. I should have a man who wants to show me off, not hide me in dark alleyways!"

"I'm working on it, dearest," he said quickly. "Once Father completes the paperwork, we will have the deed to the Sanson place. I told you the other night, with access to the water, we won't need the Melbourne ranch."

"You say this to my face, but your father and Mrs. Melbourne are still going forward with wedding plans for you and Victoria." It was dark, but Sandra sounded furious. "How do you think that makes me feel?"

"I'm going to have a talk with Victoria as soon as she gets home. I told you about her going to visit her brother. She and I have never spoken about the wedding—not once! This arrangement is all being done by my father and her mother. When I speak to her, I'm going to tell her I love another woman."

"You were supposed to tell your father," she reminded him sternly.

"The funeral and taking over Don's ranch upset my planning," he lamented weakly. "Besides, he won't listen to anything I say. That man has a full measure of cast iron between his ears. I seriously doubt he'll hear what I'm saying until I convince Victoria to break our engagement."

"What if she refuses?" Sandra asked. "You said her feelings didn't matter, that this was all her mother's doing. What if she has no choice but to go through with the wedding?"

"I can't answer that," was his lame reply. "I told you before, I hardly know her. I've seldom spoken to her, other than in passing at a party or social function. The two of us have never done any courting—hell, we've never even danced together."

"Nor have we," Sandra reminded him.

"But we will," he said quickly. "You'll see. Soon as we have a clear deed to the Sanson range, I'll talk to Victoria and ask her to call off the wedding. When she defies her mother's wishes, Father won't have any choice. He will have to let go of the notion of owning the whole valley. The idea of any marriage contract between me and Victoria will be dismissed."

"Excuse me if I don't trust your logic, Winston. Victoria might not be able to stand up to her mother any more than you can to Malcolm. I'm told Mrs. Melbourne is like your father—both have wills of iron—and you admit that your father's greed knows no bounds. I don't think he will be satisfied until he controls every head of cattle and all of the land in this part of the country."

Winston wished to remain positive. If he could convince Sandra, perhaps he could convince himself. But the girl was too smart. When he reached for her, she stepped away. She wasn't going to let him hold her close again, not so long as he was engaged to be married to another woman.

"I'll find a way," he promised her. "I swear, Sandra, I'll find a way."

"Until you do, I don't want you holding me in your arms, and I don't want you kissing me." It sounded as if the girl was near tears. "It only makes things harder."

Winston tried to figure a way to reassure her and ease her worries, but he had nothing convincing on his side. The best shot for him was how Victoria felt about this whole matrimonial decision. She was being coerced to save the family's ranch, but he could work around that. If their herd was doing well this year, they might be able to make the mortgage payment. In a matter of two or three years, they would be out of debt. He had to speak to her and see if they couldn't work this out. She wouldn't want to marry someone who loved another person. It stood to reason that the two of them could find a way out of this mess.

He tried once more to explain his logic to Sandra, but she maintained her distance.

"I want to be courted properly . . . out in the open. No more hiding, no more sneaking around," she vowed.

Winston's shoulders drooped in defeat. "I understand, Sandra. I'll do everything I can to make it happen."

"I . . . I do want to be with you," she murmured softly. "You know how I feel." At his nod, she finished,

"But I can't keep meeting you like a back-street harlot. I won't!"

"Yes, my love, I understand," was all Winston could think of to say. He cursed his weakness as he walked away, but he had never been able to stand up to Malcolm. The man oozed power and control. He had dominated Winston all of his life. Each time he dared challenge the man, he had been beaten down like a disciplined pup. He feared this would be no different. His objections to the union with Victoria would fall upon the deaf ears of the dogmatic tyrant he called Father. Equally intimidating was Martha Melbourne. It was likely that Victoria would have as much trouble going against her tyrant mother.

Father should have married her! he though sourly. *Together, they could have conquered the world!*

Victoria sat on the porch alongside Avery. It was the first time they had been completely alone.

"Guess you're heading back tomorrow?" Avery spoke up.

"I enjoyed doing nothing all day yesterday, but three nights away—Mom will be expecting us before dark tomorrow."

"Long ride to make in one day."

"We'll start before it gets light. Mrs. Butters is a sound horse. She's made the trip in one day before."

"I remember when she was a colt," he said. "She used to follow you around like a puppy."

Victoria smiled at the memory. "I think it was so she could steal my sandwiches."

"Don't give me that, sis; you used to steal butter from the kitchen and feed it to her."

She laughed. "Mother caught me one time, and I about got a beating."

"Never happened." He dismissed the notion. "You were mom's little flower, the most precious girl in the world. She never tired of dressing you up and showing you off."

"Maybe not for her, but it certainly got old for me."

"And now you're betrothed to Winston Vanderpool, son of the wealthiest man in the county."

"I've only met him a couple of times. Mother was in such a rush to make a deal with Malcolm, she threw me at him like an ante at the start of a game of cards. I can't believe she is bartering me like a horse."

Avery lowered his head. "It isn't all about you, kid." He sighed. "I'm partly to blame."

"What are you talking about?"

"Sis, I was the one Mom counted on to take over the ranch. Father was never much of a ranch manager. He ran it, gave the orders to the hired hands, but it was Mom who did all of the head work. She kept the budget, paid the bills, and decided how to keep the place going. As much as she wants you to marry someone of social merit, she needs to find a way to keep the ranch solvent."

"I know we lost a sizable portion of the herd last year to sickness, but the cattle are healthy this year. We'll be able to catch up in a couple of years."

"They might not be facing foreclosure on the mortgage, but the debt is fairly large, and managing a ranch takes a lot of energy and time. I think Mom has grown tired, and with Father suffering a stroke, she might be looking to turn all of the ranch problems over to someone else."

"Like Malcolm and his son."

"And then there's this place too."

Her eyebrows arched inquisitively. "This place?"

"The folks used their savings and even borrowed some money to help me get set up. I'm working toward the day I can begin to repay them, but we had to buy livestock, grain, and hay, then added on more rooms. I've used every dime I've made for growth and improvements. This place is making money—it's going to make a lot of money—but I can't begin to pay the folks back for the next year or two."

"So Mom and Dad need a merger—I believe that's what this is called," she said bitterly. "I'm part of a negotiation, a settlement, a payment for marrying the most eligible bachelor in the county."

"It isn't all that bad, is it?" he asked. "I hear Winston is running for mayor and is a cinch to win." Avery showed some enthusiasm. "Think of it, Sis, you'll be secure and live in a fine house, perhaps even move. Winston might become a senator or even governor."

Victoria was suddenly very tired, depressed, and unable to continue their conversation. Her worth as a person was no more than a framed picture in a store window with a sign saying FOR SALE above it. Her life was not her own—it belonged to her mother, something with which she could barter a deal or secure the ranch's future. The remaining herd of cattle had more worth than her. And the worst of it was, she had come to ask Avery's advice, get his counseling on how to escape a wedding she didn't want, only to learn that his own debts had contributed to her woes. He needed her to marry Winston to keep from losing his business.

"I'd better get off to bed," she told Avery, rising to her feet. "I'm sure Cullen will have everything ready to go by the time I get up."

"If you'd like, I can have the cook wake you. He starts preparing breakfast well before daylight."

"Yes, thank you, Avery. That's a good idea."

"It's been great seeing you, sis. I hope everything works out for you." He said the words, but there was a helplessness and a measure of guilt buried within his eyes.

"And for you too, big brother," she replied.

He might have said good night, but she no longer heard the words. Victoria was in a trance, walking toward her room like a wooden soldier, wishing her heart might turn to stone. If she felt nothing, she could marry Winston and be content. Not happy, but content.

Chapter Six

Concho reached the old trail and traveled along it for twenty miles. His pal, Stoker, kept pace with him, riding at his side, but the man had never been much for small talk.

"Even after the rain, you can see it's a single-horse buggy," Concho reported, tipping his head toward the hoof-prints they were following. "That will make them easy to stop."

"Too bad the Indians have been moved to reservations," Stoker said. "We could make it look like a random attack if there were still renegades running loose."

"A couple of wandering bandits will have to do."

"Whatever you say, Joe."

Concho didn't reply to that—Stoker was the only man alive who still called him Joe. He had used a pseudonym since he started doing select jobs several years back. His new title was chosen because it afforded him a reputation but not recognition. Word got around—if a person had a problem, faced opposition, or needed to be rid of someone, Concho would take care of it. Stoker and he had been a team for ten years. They had ridden the river and escaped more than one posse together. Stoker had never changed from calling him by his old first name. As for the men he hired out to—men who wanted a job done for money and didn't ask personal questions—they knew him only as Concho.

"Looks as if they turned off the trail here," Stoker observed, tipping his head toward a narrow side trail. "The markings are from before the storm. Why would they do that?"

"I'll bet it's where they spent the night."

"Joe, you think they might figure to stay there again on the way back?"

"We won't count on it. They might have gotten a late start going over. The inn is forty to fifty miles." He looked around slowly. "I'd say this is about the halfway mark. They probably went up the creek a bit and found a cove or glen where they could stay the night."

"Let's check it out," Stoker offered.

"Good idea. We've got plenty of time."

The pair rode along the trail until they reached a campsite. The fire pit was surrounded by rocks, and the ground was still damp from the previous rain.

"Take a look over there," Stoker said, indicating a narrow gorge. "Looks like a piece of canvas or a tent."

They moved to the edge of the creek—there was a mere trickle of water running—and looked at the tangle of blankets and canvas half buried in a pile of sticks and debris.

"Wonder if anyone was in that when it got washed down here," Stoker said. "I'd guess one of the tents was pitched too close to the stream."

"Flash flood from the heavy rain," Concho observed.

"This would be a good place for us to surprise them."

Concho took a long look around. "Only if they decided to come up here again. If they were the ones who lost the tent, they probably intend on making the trip home in one day. We'll ride a bit farther along the main trail and see if there is a good spot for an ambush. If not, we can take them back down at the entrance to the cove. I remember seeing cover on both sides of the trail."

"Lead on, Joe," Stoker replied. "You're the man with the head for this sort of ambush."

The ride back had an ominous feel to it. They left after an early breakfast and were on the trail well before sunup. Victoria had been bright and cheerful around her brother's family, but she was withdrawn and sullen on the return trip. Cully wondered how much of her dark mood could be attributed to what lay ahead—her marriage to Winston Vanderpool.

"You made a good impression." Her speaking up startled Cully. He removed his gaze from the trail and glanced at her.

"Avery seems a top hand in every sense, Sparks." He reciprocated the praise. "I can see why you have such a high opinion of him."

She smiled at his observation. "Dad called him that

from the time he could walk—his little *top hand*, or, *Avery will be my* top hand *one day*. Nothing was too good for his *top hand,* he'd say. I was a little jealous of how Dad doted on Avery. He naturally thought my brother would run the ranch one day."

"But Avery didn't like working cattle?"

Victoria sighed. "No. Although it didn't all have to do with the cattle. He couldn't work around my mother. She is a very controlling type of person. She was continually after him to continue his education, and she arranged for him to meet certain girls—she tried to run his life. He fled to get away from her as much as to start his own life."

"Maybe you ought to follow his example."

Her expression became stern. "I'm not being forced to wed at gunpoint, Mr. Lomax. The marriage was arranged, but I am not without some voice in my future."

"Really?" He was intentionally impertinent. "Seems to me you're being driven to this here wedding like a horse to a branding chute."

"You'd best mind your tongue, if you care to remain in our employ," she said with some vigor. "My mother— though she is willful and a bit pompous—has always wanted what is best for me."

Cully returned to watching the horse and the trail ahead. He didn't care to get into a row he could not win. If the girl was willing to give up her future to please her mother, it was none of his affair. He would keep shed of an argument and—

He pulled suddenly back on the reins. The abrupt

stop nearly unseated Victoria. She swung about and glared at him.

"What on earth are you . . . ?"

Cully shushed her, holding up a hand to stop her question. Before she could ask what he was up to, he climbed down from the buggy and walked to the front of the rig. He took a few moments to walk back and forth along the faint trail. When he returned to the carriage, Victoria regarded him with a look of concern.

"What is it?" she asked in a hushed voice.

Cully took a careful look around, then removed his gun and added a sixth round to fill the lone empty chamber. He had been riding with the rawhide thong holding the pistol in place, but now he left it off, keeping the gun ready for instant use.

"There are fresh tracks from a couple of riders—I'd guess not more than a couple of hours back. The hard rain removed all other tracks on the trail except for our own. For some reason those two horsemen came this far and turned around."

Victoria pivoted slowly on the wagon cushion and searched the surrounding area. "Why would they do that? There's not a house or ranch around here for miles."

"It could be nothing," Cully said, climbing back into the runabout, "but I don't like it." He gave her a serious look. "If any kind of trouble starts, you get down on the floorboards and stay as low as you can."

"Cully, you're scaring me."

He tried to put her mind at ease. "It might only be a couple of wandering hunters or a pair of cowboys who decided to change directions. This trail isn't used by many, but there are bound to be a few who know it's here."

"Except most people take the main trail," she replied. "We came this way because our ranch sits several miles off of the main road."

Cully took up the reins and started the horse moving again. His gaze swept across the rolling hills and probed both sides of the trail, watching for movement or danger.

"Just stay alert, and be ready to duck. There's no reason to expect trouble, but it won't hurt to be prepared."

Victoria's hand came to rest on his arm. "Maybe we should go back. We could take the longer route back home. The tracks could be from a couple of bandits on the run. Perhaps they saw us coming and turned around."

"It's only two horses, and they are well shod. Men on the run don't usually have time to get their horses new shoes. Plus they were riding slow and easy before turning around, so they weren't worried about a posse." He continued his surveillance. "As for our turning back for the inn, if those two are after us, they could easily overtake us from behind. It's best we go forward and see what lies ahead."

"All right, if you say so," she decided. "If we push Mrs. Butters, we can be home in another six hours. Mother will start to worry if we don't get there by dark."

"I don't know." Cully attempted to lighten the mood. "I was kind of looking forward to sharing a tent with you again."

"You'd better never mention that when anyone else can hear," she warned. "I still haven't decided how to tell Father about our losing one of the tents."

"I'll say it was mine, and the wind blew it over in the storm. Rather than try to put it back up, I chucked it into the creek."

"That makes you sound like a wild man with a temper," she mused, "but I've never seen you angry. You're about the most temperate man I've ever known."

"I get riled on occasion, but a man shouldn't ought to show his bad side in the presence of a lady."

She giggled. *"Shouldn't ought?"* she repeated. "Did I once say you sounded educated?"

He started to grin, but the horse suddenly reared.

A gunshot sounded as the animal left its feet. "Down!" Cully commanded Victoria as Mrs. Butters crumpled to the ground.

Cully had his gun out before Victoria could start to duck for cover. He instantly spied the smoke from the rifle barrel not a hundred feet away and fired off three quick shots—one at the smoke and one to either side.

A man staggered from behind the tall sagebrush and toppled onto his face.

Cully felt the wind from a second bullet—it missed his head by inches.

Whirling in that direction, he followed the sound from the blast of the gun and returned fire to the opposite side of the trail. A man in the bushes yelped from being hit by Cully's second of three rounds and quickly disappeared over a small rise. A moment later there came the sound of two horses running hard, the sound fading as the distance increased.

The silence and gunfire caused a ringing in Cully's ears while he quickly reloaded his pistol. A glance told him that Victoria was all right, and he jumped down. He kept his gun ready, cocked for immediate use.

His caution was unnecessary. The first attacker was lying facedown, with his head turned to one side. His eyes and mouth were both wide open. The bullet had hit him between the eyes, though it was well off center. Obviously, the fellow had still been sighting down the barrel of his rifle when Cully fired at the smoke. He counted it a blessing that the man's first shot had been at the horse to stop the carriage. Had he aimed at Cully or Victoria instead . . .

"He's dead?" Victoria's voice brought him back to the present. She had gotten out of the runabout and was a few feet behind him.

"Doubt he had time to know he'd lost the fight."

"Poor Mrs. Butters," the girl lamented, suppressing a sob of grief. "I raised her from a colt. She was my favorite pet."

"I'm real sorry, Sparks," Cully said. "She seemed a fine animal."

"Not an animal," she said, tears slipping down her cheeks. "She was my truest friend."

"Mrs. Butters . . . strange name for a horse," he said, pausing to glance back at her.

"As a foal she was always mooching food," Victoria explained, her voice soft and filled with sorrow. "She raided a picnic basket one time and stole an entire block of butter—I also lost more than one sandwich to her. I called her Butters until she had a colt of her own. Then I changed her name to match her status."

"Hence the name *Mrs*. Butters."

"I'm glad she didn't suffer."

"More than that, she saved our lives." At Victoria's tearful puzzlement, he explained. "When she reared up, it ruined the second shooter's aim. By the time Mrs. Butters went down, I was able to shoot back. The second man missed me because the situation had changed. He wasn't prepared for a real fight and ran for his life when I began to return fire."

"Why would anyone attack us?"

"I have no idea."

She eyed him with unmasked suspicion. "You're more than a handyman," she said. "I think perhaps someone is out to kill you."

"I can't imagine who."

"A robbery?" she asked. "Could they have intended to rob us?"

Cully had no idea and told her so.

"What do we do now?"

"Can't take this guy's body with us, and the coyotes and such will be at him before we can get back. I'll check him for identification and use the shovel we packed with the overnight gear to bury him."

"Then we start walking," Victoria deduced. "We won't make it to the ranch tonight on foot. It's close to twenty miles."

Cully took a quick survey of the sky. "Not a cloud anywhere," he said. "We can carry food and water, along with a couple of blankets. Looks as if I'll get to sleep next to you one more time after all."

"Not the romantic interlude you had hoped, I'm sure."

"The romantic—what kind of *lude*?"

She let it pass. "What do you need me to do?"

"You put together what we need to carry with us. Soon as I plant this jasper, we'll bundle everything into blankets and fashion some straps so we can carry them on our backs."

Victoria didn't argue. She reached out and tenderly patted the dead horse, then started to work. Cully removed a short-handled shovel from the buggy and looked for some soft earth. They needed to get moving before the second shooter changed his mind and returned to finish the job.

Concho stopped after a couple of miles and stared back the way he'd come. His heart was heavy, and a stinging burned his eyes. He blinked back the tears angrily. Stoker had ridden at his side for so long, he'd been like a younger brother to him. He was the closest thing to family Concho had.

And that damned handyman killed him!

The chore should have been simple. He'd had a bead on the driver, ready to put a bullet through his heart. But Stoker's shot caused the horse to rear and ruined his chance. The horse went down at an angle, and it caused the buggy to turn sideways enough that he couldn't get a clear shot. He'd fired out of desperation but too late to save Stoker's life.

He had seen his friend go down and knew he was dead. The driver had been deadly and very fast with his gun. That was not something he had expected. Few men traveled rough terrain without securing their gun in its holster. Yet this guy had brought his pistol into play before the horse even hit the ground. It was as if he'd been warned they were waiting in ambush.

He cursed such insane logic. How could the driver have known he was riding into a trap? Both horses had been hidden in the draw behind him, and he knew Stoker had not given away his position until he shot the horse. So how did the man react so quickly? He replayed the scene in his head. The girl had dropped out of sight immediately, much too quickly for an ordinary passenger to react. They were more than ready; they had somehow anticipated an attack.

Concho started his horse moving, tugging on the reins to bring along Stoker's gelding. The easy money for this job suddenly was not worth the price. It was going to take a new plan to get this done, and he would need more men. He had made a deal that included an ordinary ranch hand, but the man driving the buggy was anything but ordinary. And Stoker had paid the ultimate price for Concho's lack of accurate information.

"I'm damn sorry, pard," he said aloud. "But rest easy

in your grave—that man won't live long enough to enjoy his victory today."

The bundles were not really comfortable as backpacks, but Cully secured them in place with short pieces of tent cord. Victoria carried the lighter pack, but she was not used to such physical work. As darkness covered the land, Cully could tell she was struggling to keep walking.

"Let's hole up between those boulders," he said, indicating a patch of ground between two rock formations. "We'll keep a cold camp, in case the second ambusher is somewhere nearby."

"You think he might try to get at us during the night?"

"I'll keep watch," Cully replied.

"You have to sleep too."

"It won't hurt for me to skip a night's sleep, Sparks."

"Well, I'll rest for a bit and then let you get some sleep too. I don't want you stumbling around half-awake and have that attacker surprise us tomorrow."

He didn't argue, leading the way to the small clearing. He dropped his pack and helped Victoria with hers. She arched her back and flexed her shoulders, once the heavy bundle was removed.

"I'm going to be stiff for a week from this long trek."

Cully spread out the blankets before he set about making their supper. Two tins of beans, a chunk of cornmeal cake—thoughtfully provided by Avery's wife—and an airtight jar of peaches. Opening the cans was the extent of his preparation.

"Avery married a good cook," Cully said, savoring the tasty cake. "What about you?"

Victoria paused between bites. "What about me?"

"Can you cook, or are you going to have a housekeeper and cook do all of your chores for you after you're married?"

"I'll have you know I've been tutored in preparing meals, along with formal etiquette and a multitude of other domestic subjects. I'm as educated as many of the girls who attend a woman's or co-educational college for two or three years."

"Of course you are."

She frowned. "At least I haven't done anything to have someone out trying to kill me!"

"You think they were after me?"

Victoria laughed at the absurdity of his question. "I would imagine you have a thousand enemies—being that you are such a mischievous rogue. As for me, I've not an enemy in the entire world."

"They shot our horse so we couldn't run," Cully pointed out. "That could mean they intended to shoot us both. A couple of robbers would have blocked the trail and covered us from horseback. They didn't need to show themselves, just force us to hand over everything we had. The attack today seemed more like an ambush than a robbery."

"How do you know so much about it?"

"What if I told you I used to be a deputy U.S. Marshal?"

"I'd try not to laugh"—she snickered—"though un-successfully."

"How about an assistant to the Colorado Attorney General's office?"

"Not buying it."

"A Federal agent?"

"Nor that either."

"All right, how about a Pinkerton Eye?"

She sighed wearily. "Perhaps a gunrunner or snake-oil salesman—that I would accept." At his frown, she included, "Or a paltry, small-time criminal on the run. Did you get caught stealing chickens, sparking with a married man's wife, cheating at cards?"

"Dad-gum! You really believe I'm such a complete failure that I couldn't have at least committed a real crime?"

She laughed. "You're a shiftless handyman with no ambition. What else should I think about you?"

He shook his head. "If I'm so worthless as a human being, why would anyone want to kill me?"

"The sneaking off to court another man's wife could have an angry husband after you."

Cully beamed a good-natured grin. "At least you fig-ure I could attract a woman, married or not—that's some-thing."

"You attracted a couple of killers too."

He had finished eating but mentally chewed on what little they knew. Two men had set a professional ambush. The dead man had no papers on him, not so much as a single coin in his pockets. That meant they had stowed everything on their horses, a natural precaution in case one of them was killed. With the second man getting away, he hadn't a clue as to who the shooters were, nor the reason behind the attack.

"You look as if you're thinking very hard about something," Victoria interrupted. "Might give yourself a headache doing something so uncharacteristic."

He chuckled at her spunk but was serious when he spoke. "Finish up and turn in. You need to get some sleep."

Chapter Seven

Concho spied the man he wanted to talk to. He knew that the gent often hung around the saloon or casino. He waited—it took only a minute before Concho caught the man's eye—and signaled him with a tip of his head toward the door and walked out into the dark night. His employer caught up a couple of minutes later, and they moved into a dark alleyway to talk.

"Job done?" the man asked.

"You sent me hunting rabbits with a slingshot, my good friend, and we wound up in a foul-tempered grizzly bear's den!" Concho did not conceal his ire. "You didn't tell us we were taking on a deadly gunman."

"What are you talking about?"

"I never saw a quicker or more lethal man with a gun. That guy used a six-iron like he'd been trained by the devil himself. Killed Stoker in an instant and took a chunk out of my arm before I had a chance to take aim." Concho swore and showed him the bandage around his upper arm. "You should have warned us about him!"

"But I didn't know," the man whined. "I had no idea he was some kind of fast-gun artist!"

"Stoker was in the brush, completely hidden from sight, and the man hit him square. He nicked me too— must have figured where I was from the sound of my first and only shot. I'm damn lucky to still be breathing. That man is walking death! You paid us to bushwhack a couple of ordinary people out for an afternoon ride, and we end up facing the deadliest gun in the Territory!"

"I tell you, I didn't know! The guy's been working at the Melbourne place as a handyman. I didn't think he'd be a problem."

Concho wished he could see the man's face, but it was after midnight, and every place was closed and dark, save the saloon. The fellow sounded as if he was telling the truth, so Concho made an effort to quash his ire.

"It's going to take a couple more men to get the job done, especially now that the gunman will be expecting trouble. I'm going to need another two hundred to see this gets done."

"I paid for the job already. I don't think—"

Concho grabbed the front of the man's jacket. "Stoker was like a brother to me!" He snarled the words. "I'm going to kill that gunman no matter what."

"Raising the price was not part of our deal."

"I know where I can get two more men, the kind who will do anything for a buck. I'm not going to pay them out of my share, and Stoker was helping support his parents over in Denver. He earned his pay!"

"I don't know. This is getting complicated."

"You hired me to do the job, and my best friend is dead. I know a couple of men who can help to get the job done right. There's nothing complicated about it."

"All right," the man gave in. "I'll get you the money . . . after the job is done." Then, with a bit more courage in his voice, he said, "But I want this over with as soon as possible. No more mistakes."

"The 'mistake' was our not being told about the handyman's ability with a gun."

"It wasn't *my* mistake. I had no idea he would be a problem."

Concho released his grip on the man's jacket. He needed a bottle and a few hours to drink and grieve over the loss of his friend. Once he had washed the hurt from his bones, he would put a plan into motion to be rid of the man named Cullen Lomax.

Victoria was completely spent from the long walk. Although she claimed she would relieve Cully, she didn't wake up until daybreak. Rather than try to take a short nap, Cully prepared what little they had for breakfast, and they ate a quick meal.

"You can't walk ten or twelve more miles without any sleep," Victoria protested. "We're going to be a day late anyway. What's the difference if you rest for a few hours?"

"The difference will be how your mother handles all of this. We need to get you home safely as quickly as possible. I can come back with a couple of horses and pick up the carriage and the other belongings. We only need to carry a little water with us and the last of our hard rolls. Everything else we can leave behind."

"I suppose you're right, but I hate the idea of your having stayed awake all night. You should have woken me up."

"It won't hurt me to miss one night's sleep, and I'm in better shape for travel than you," he said. "I'll bet you have blisters the size of pennies on both feet."

"My back and shoulders are stiff and sore too," she admitted. "I don't think I would make a very good pack animal."

"It's coming on to sunup," Cully told her. "We'll try to take it slow and easy to conserve your strength. Are you ready to get started?"

She might be prissy and prim, a delicate lady, educated, with manners and grace, yet the girl had grit. She got to her feet and picked up her canteen. "I'm ready when you are," she affirmed. "Are we going to stand around and talk or start walking?"

Cully hid the smile that played along his lips while picking up his own canteen of water. They had filled up at the creek, but that had been ten miles and twelve hours ago. They were going to be dry and thirsty before they saw the buildings of home.

The march began in earnest, but the miles started to take their toll. Victoria began to limp after a time, and soon they were stopping every few minutes. Finally, she sat down on a rock and dropped the canteen at her feet.

"Go on without me," she told Cully, hanging her

head. "It can't be but a few more miles, and you can bring back a horse."

"I would have left you at the carriage if I dared leave you alone," he told her. "We can't take the chance on that second attacker returning."

Those words caused her to look up at him. "Why would he want to hurt me?"

"I don't know," he replied. "I don't know why he and his partner tried to shoot us to start with."

She studied him for a moment. "You're telling the truth? You really don't know?"

"I've not led the life of a saint, but I settled all of my debts before I hired on with your father."

"So you claim, but it seems I've been drawn into a personal vendetta," she said. "How thoughtful of you to include me in the excitement."

"The idea of getting killed can't be as bad for you as for me," he said. "I've got my whole life ahead of me— your fate is to marry Winston Vanderpool."

"I know why you say things like that," she countered. "You're jealous of him."

"Winston has nothing in the world I want." Cully put a meaningful look on Victoria. "Not yet anyway."

His candor brought a bit of color into the girl's cheeks, but her feisty disposition surfaced. "Hah!" she said triumphantly. "You *do* have romantic notions about me. I knew it!"

"Hardly a surprise, Sparks. You're the prettiest gal I ever laid eyes on. You're smart, have a sense of humor, and, when I held you in my arms, it felt like the most natural thing in the world."

She gasped at his boldness and sprang to her feet. "W-When . . . When . . ." she sputtered. "Cullen Lomax! When you held me in your arms, it was for warmth and comfort. There was not one single thing 'romantic' about it."

"Felt pretty romantic to me," he countered, displaying a confident grin. "You can say what you want, but I think you felt it too."

"I don't have to listen to this insanity," she lashed out. "I can darn well walk as long as you can!"

Cully kept pace with her. She started off at a brisk pace, but he could tell that every step hurt her. When she stumbled and nearly went down, he was quick to grab hold of her arm to prevent a fall. She twisted about, only to end up facing him, wrapped within his embrace and gazing directly into his eyes.

"Marrying someone you don't love is the biggest mistake you could make, Sparks," Cully said gently. "No woman should be bartered to a man because he's rich; she should marry someone who will treasure and love her with an undying devotion."

Victoria's lips parted, as if she would speak, but no words came forth. At her hesitation, Cully did what any man—whose brain had been bewitched by a goddess—would do. He kissed her.

The world stood still, as if nothing else existed other than the delight of holding and kissing this most desirable of all women. Rather than resist or fight his boldness, Victoria surrendered to him. It was the most amazing feeling Cully had ever imagined. They might have continued forever, except for one little thing. . . .

"What on earth—? Cullen Lomax!" A shrill screech split the tranquil afternoon. "Get your filthy hands off of my daughter this minute!"

Cully let go of Victoria as if he had mistakenly hugged a white-hot stove. He backed up so fast, he tripped over a clump of sagebrush and fell, landing on his back pockets and elbows.

"Mother!" Victoria exclaimed, whirling about, red-faced, to stare at her. "How did you . . . ?"

"What in heaven's name is going on?" Martha wailed. "Where have you been? Where's the carriage?"

Cully slowly rose to his feet, his shoulders squared and jaw anchored, ready to meet the firing squad. He saw that Jeff was at the helm of their buckboard. As for Martha, she had climbed down and now strode forward—an enraged bull ready to gore something or someone with her deadly horns.

Victoria quickly stepped between her mother and Cully, forcing the woman to stop before she could physically assault him.

"We were attacked," she informed her mother gravely. "Two men ambushed us yesterday, about fifteen miles back down the trail. They killed Mrs. Butters and might have killed us, except Cullen shot one of them and drove the other away."

Martha's anger was temporarily curbed by her concern. "Are you hurt?" She quickly looked Victoria up and down. "Did you get hit by the gunfire?"

"No, they missed us both."

"You say there was an ambush?" Jeff climbed down to join them, limping forward to look them both over. "What did they want?"

"There wasn't time to exchange polite conversation," Cully replied. "They killed the horse to stop the carriage, and then one of them fired a round at me."

"You think they were out to kill you, Cullen?"

"It would seem so," Cully answered. "Miss Melbourne ducked onto the floorboards, and I returned fire. I got one with a lucky shot, but the second man fled."

"Did you hear that?" Martha cried. "Jefford, I told you something was wrong."

"Yes, Martha, you were right."

"But just now"—the woman swung her furious glare at Cully—"were you, or were you not, kissing my daughter?"

It didn't sound like a question, but Cully quickly accepted blame for his actions. "I kind of forgot my manners, Mrs. Melbourne," he said. "I assure you, I didn't mean anything by it. We had an argument, and I was trying to prove a point."

"A point!" she bellowed. "What kind of point is demonstrated by forcing your attentions onto my daughter?"

"That we shouldn't separate," he improvised. "She wanted to stay behind and have me walk to the house and get help. I told her she was too vulnerable alone. . . ."

Martha showed contempt at his tale. "And the only

way to prove that was to overpower and kiss her—is that your defense?"

"Pretty much," he said lamely.

The woman's scathing stare flashed at her daughter. "Is what he says true, Victoria? Were you actually thinking of staying here alone, with some killer running loose in the hills?"

"It was my feet," the girl replied weakly, unable to meet her mother's burning stare. "I've got blisters so bad, I can hardly walk. I knew you would be worried, and I wanted to get word to you as quickly as possible."

"I would never want that at the risk of your personal safety!"

"I'm sorry, Mother. It was a silly idea."

Martha appeared to accept her story, but that didn't mean her wrath toward Cully had lessened. The fiery glare rested on him again, and she practically bored scorch marks into his forehead.

"When we get back to the house, you are to pack your things and get off of our ranch. Do you understand me, Mr. Lomax?"

"Yes, ma'am, I hear you."

"Mother, please!" Victoria tried to intervene.

"The subject is not open for discussion!" she said vehemently. "Can you walk as far as the wagon?"

Victoria's shoulders sagged in defeat. "Yes, Mother."

Jeff continued to frown. Like Martha, he was horror-struck at the idea of the handyman's putting his daughter into harm's way.

"You'll ride in the wagon bed," Jeff told Cully. "I'll speak to you back at the house."

"Yes, sir," Cully replied.

Once everyone was aboard, Cully sat on the hard wooden bed and tried to keep his innards from being churned out of him by the rough and rutted trail. He suffered the regret of having been caught kissing Victoria, but, worse than that, there hadn't been time to measure her reaction. She hadn't fought or resisted his advance in the slightest. Quite the opposite—she'd seemed to return a portion of his ardor. However, the arrival of Jeff and Martha had eliminated any chance to follow up on her reaction.

You sure handled this well, old buddy, he told himself. *The only chance you'll ever have to discover how the girl feels about you, and you get caught red-handed by her mother!*

Victoria relished soaking in the hot water. The bath relieved some of the ache in her bones, though her feet burned from her numerous blisters. She sank down into the tub and closed her eyes. She might have dozed off, jaded from the long walk, sleeping on the hard ground, and then bouncing about on the buckboard for four hours. However, she could not get Cully out of her head. Why had he kissed her? And, to her chagrin, why had she not resisted?

It made no sense. He had always been a perfect gentleman—a teaser, yes, but never had he hinted that he might do something so incredibly rash. She clung to that notion as her excuse for not fighting him off.

I could have stopped him, had I offered up the slightest resistance, she thought. *Is it possible I wanted him to kiss me?*

It was entirely possible. She had seen desire in his eyes on numerous occasions, although his manner and speech never crossed the line. At least it hadn't . . . until he chose the exact wrong moment to kiss her.

What if Mother had not arrived? she wondered. Would she have found the strength to resist the wonderful bliss of being held close and kissed with such an honest passion? Would she have restored her feminine virtue by slapping him? Or would she have wantonly invited him to kiss her a second time?

She ruefully dismissed the unanswerable questions and forced her mind to other puzzles. She wondered again about the ambush. Cully had seen the warning signs, deduced from a few markings on the ground that they might be headed for trouble. He had seen to her safety, instructing her to get down out of harm's way, while he bravely shot it out with two assailants. He had killed one and driven off the second man. He had shown more than mere courage; he was definitely more than the simple handyman he pretended to be.

Thinking back, when she had asked him what his profession had been before he came to the ranch, his answers had been ridiculous: a detective, a government agent, a deputy marshal. . . . She frowned in thought. What if he had been telling the truth? Was it possible that he *had* worked at one of those jobs, and she had waved it off as another of his wild tales?

The door suddenly opened, and Martha stood at the entrance. She had a small container and some strips of cloth in her hands.

"Soon as you're done, I'll tend to those nasty blisters," she offered.

"I want to wash my hair," Victoria replied. "I'll be a few more minutes."

Martha gave an affirmative nod but did not leave. "It's for the best," she said, clearly speaking of Cully's dismissal.

Victoria met her stare. "He saved my life, Mother."

"He endangered your life!" she shot back. "Those assassins who were after him could have killed you!"

"I'm talking about before the attack, Mother." At the woman's puzzled look, she recounted her near drowning. "He pulled me from the rushing water; he saved my life."

Her mother absorbed that information, and her features softened minutely. "I can understand how you might have developed an . . . appreciation for the man," she allowed, choosing her words carefully, "but nothing can come of it."

"He protected me. He saved my life at the risk of his own! What more could you ask?"

"That he not put you in danger in the first place," she fired back. "Nearly drowning is your own fault for insisting you had to visit Avery. We could have made arrangements for you to see him, but, no, you had to do it on your own."

"I needed time alone, peace and quiet, a chance to think."

"Think about what?" her mother snapped. "A life with a handyman?"

"He would make me a better husband and appreciate me more than Winston," she fired right back. "Cullen said a man should treasure a woman and do everything in his power to make her happy. Winston is going to expect *me* to be the one to treasure *him*!"

"He'll be an important man one day, Victoria. First mayor, then a senator or congressman—perhaps even governor of the state!"

"Is that what's important in life, Mother, a title in front of your name? A bigger house than your neighbor, endless social gatherings where you compare who has the most dazzling jewelry and clothing, or who hires the most servants? What about love and happiness? Don't those things count for anything?"

"Being poor wouldn't make you happy, nor would seeing us lose the ranch."

"And being married to a man I don't love—is that supposed to make me happy?"

"I don't see why we have to go over this same argument every few days. You agreed to marry Winston for the sake of us all. The announcement has been made."

"I never 'agreed' to anything," Victoria countered. "You told me it was all arranged—you and Malcolm Vanderpool decided I was to marry his son. I never got to voice an opinion, and I doubt Winston did either."

"It's what is best for us all."

"So long as I keep my mouth shut and agree to do whatever you tell me to." Victoria continued to present her case. "Do you want to know why Cullen was kissing me?" She glared hot spikes at her mother. "It's because I let him!" Her mother's complexion darkened with her ire, but she held her temper. "It's probably the only time in my life I will be kissed by a man who wants me because of who I am . . . not because I'm part of a contract to seal a bargain!"

"Enough of this silly chatter, Victoria," the woman barked sharply. "The marriage between you and Winston will solidify our ranch as never before. We will merge our holdings with Malcolm's and have the largest ranch in all of Wyoming."

Victoria was cynical. "How wonderful for you."

Her mother's face darkened, and Victoria knew that civil dialogue had ended. When Martha spoke again, her teeth were clenched, the way they always were when she grew furious yet refrained from screaming at the top of her lungs.

"I'll leave these things for you," she said tightly, placing the jar and cloths on the dresser. "If you need some help, you only have to call out. Otherwise, I'll be downstairs"—scorn entered her tone—"making out wedding invitations."

Victoria endured in silence the rush of anger that flooded her being. Doing verbal battle with her mother was futile. She was a mouse shaking her fist at the cat while in the process of being devoured. Her fate was not in her own hands . . . it never had been.

Chapter Eight

Once Mrs. Butters was free of her harness, Cully used his horse and rope to pull the animal from the trail. The replacement carriage horse was the one Jeff Melbourne had been riding. The ranch boss moved slowly, perceptibly stiff from the ride.

"You should have let me come back alone," Cully said. "Either that or sent someone else. This ride has to be hell on your aching bones."

"Doc told me a good many younger men would have died from the stroke. I'm not the kind to go down without a fight."

"Neither am I, Jeff." Yet Cully displayed a helpless expression. "I made a mistake kissing your daughter, but I wasn't trying to take advantage of her."

"No?"

Cully didn't know how else to say it, so he went with the truth. "I'm pretty sure I'm in love with her."

"She is promised to Winston Vanderpool. Martha and Malcolm have already made the official announcement."

"She doesn't love him."

"I suppose she told you this?"

"Not in so many words, but she made it clear that the marriage is an arrangement between Malcolm and your wife."

Jeff didn't speak for a time, working with Cully to remove the saddle from his horse and put the animal into harness. He needed a helping hand to get up onto the wagon seat. Then he stopped to look at Cully.

"I can't offer you any advice, son," he said finally. "Martha's folks owned this ranch before we got married. When they passed on, Martha suggested we change the name of the place, but the deed is in her family's name, not mine."

"I knew she ran the business end of things, Jeff."

"Yep, and she has worked and maneuvered to pick the most eligible man in the county for our daughter. I have my say from time to time, like settling a family dispute or hiring and firing of our ranch hands, but she still makes the business decisions."

"She's quite a woman," Cully conceded.

"She's been a faithful wife, and I've loved her since we first met." He shrugged his bony shoulders. "I know she can be as mean and ornery as a wolverine, but her decisions are usually made with foresight and deliberation. She chose Winston because he is going to rise above the norm, be somebody. Plus, with the loss of so many cattle last year and helping Avery with his business, we went deeply into debt. This wedding will erase those bills."

"So you're in favor of this union?"

"Personally, I care more about Victoria's happiness," Jeff replied. "As for the joining of our ranches, once my daughter is married to Winston, we'll have no standing of our own other than as partners. If Malcolm tells his boy to sell off all of our beef and retire us both, he will have the authority to do it."

"Maybe you ought to take a stand on the issue, Jeff."

"The doctor said to avoid stressful situations." He showed a toothy grin. "Course, he told me not to do a lot of riding about the countryside too."

"Yeah, I didn't help there."

"Why do you figure these two guys were after you?"

"I have no idea, Jeff. I can't imagine how they knew where to find me. This trail—no one uses it since the stage route was mapped out several years back." Cully waved a hand in a helpless gesture. "And I've been thinking on it since the ambush. I can't imagine any enemies from the past who could have followed me here. I left my old life behind."

"I never did tell Martha the truth about you," Jeff said. "If she had known who you were, she might have balked at having you work for us. I was going to ask you to look into the sickness that killed off half of our beef, but the stroke . . . then learning to walk again. . . ." Again he shrugged his skinny shoulders. "I never got around to asking."

"You did me a favor giving me the job, Jeff," Cully told the man. "If I had thought someone was after me, I never would have hired on with you. The last thing in the world I would ever do is to put you or your family into danger."

"What are you going to do next, Cully?"

"I'll try to discover who the other guy was who ambushed me. Someone must know who was riding with the man I buried. I've got a complete description of the dead man—he had a knife scar on the cleft of his chin. If the pair asked around to find me, it might have drawn attention. I only need to find one person who remembers them to point me in the right direction."

"I hope you don't mind, but I told Sheriff Weathers you might be able to help with a murder."

"What murder?"

Jeff recounted what little they knew about Don Sanson's death.

"Someone shot down Don in cold blood?"

"No one saw or heard anything, and Don wasn't even wearing a gun. It was an execution, a murder of the worst kind."

"That sickness you mentioned last year, it only hit Don's and your herds of cattle. Why do you think it missed infecting Vanderpool's beef?"

"We share the same boundaries, Sanson and us, but Vanderpool's spread is quite a distance. I suppose none of our cattle ever got close enough to pass the disease on to his animals."

"With Don dead, you figure Malcolm will take over Sanson's ranch?"

"It's already in the works. Don took out a mortgage to keep from losing his place last year. Malcolm, by virtue of holding the deed, can write himself in as the new owner."

"That gives him a ranch half-again as big as your own."

"Yes, although I'm not sure it's big enough to suit him. He strikes me as a man who, if given the entire world, would want to lay claim to the moon." Jeff sighed. "I don't foresee him putting a stop to the wedding, though. I think he'll want our place too."

"So you want me to talk to the sheriff and offer my help in solving Don's murder?"

"He's in over his head on this kind of thing, Cully. I don't know if you can find out anything or not, but it's the right thing to do."

"Doesn't change anything between us—I'm still fired, right?"

The old boy laughed. "Yep, you're still fired."

Concho eyed the two men and hid his distaste. They called themselves hunters, but he knew they were the lowest form of animals. The two men preyed on their own kind. Robbery, blackmail, murder—it made no difference. Some would have put him into the same category, but he wasn't a common thief or killer; he was . . . an artist. He took pride in his work and assured his employer satisfaction—something yet to be achieved with this latest assignment.

"A hundred each," he told the pair. "Payment will be made when I see the man dead."

"A handyman, says you," Gunther drawled. "But he done shot yer pard?"

"Sounds gun-handy to me," Finn chimed in. "We ain't of a mind to get ourselves kilt fer a few dollars."

"Stoker and me were taken by surprise." Concho made up a story. "This guy was looking for a fight and picked my lifelong friend. He killed him without giving him a chance. I wasn't able to get my gun into play before he shot me too." He touched the bandage on his right upper arm. Though it was only scratched, he feigned a grimace when he moved it. "This here is why I can't do the job myself. Can't lift my gun arm yet."

"Be this here not something for the law to handle?" Finn asked.

"Stoker managed to get his gun out before he died. It was ruled a fair fight."

"Be it a fair fight you be looking fer from us?" Gunther asked. "We can put this lame horse down, but we'll not be riskin' a face-to-face."

"You do the job—makes no never mind how you do it—and then you pick up your pay and skedaddle. No one is going to point a finger at you, not if you do this right."

"An ambush, says he," Gunther said, grinning at his partner. "Sounds like our kind of job. Ain't that right, Finn?"

"You be telling the truth, Gun. Where do we find this here handyman?"

"He'll be coming into Elk City either today or to-morrow. I'd suggest catching him out in the open before he reaches the main street of town. There are a couple good places up the road a bit with good cover for an ambush."

"You'd best keep the money handy," Finn told Concho. "Once that polecat drops, we'll be wanting to head for the wild and unsettled."

"I'll have your money ready for you. Just make sure you do the job right."

"How will we know this fellow?"

"He wears a black, flat-crown Stetson. And I'm told his horse is a big roan with a blaze streak down the forehead and white stockings all around—prettiest mount in the county."

"And you say he's coming to town?"

"I got word he no longer has a job working at the Melbourne place. He should be showing up anytime."

"We'll be a-sittin' right here waitin' fer him," said Gunther. "Best have a wooden box sorted out fer his restin' place."

Concho bid them good luck, and the two ragged brutes left. The smell of dried blood lingered. Concho wondered if it was the blood of an animal they had butchered or the blood of the last person they had killed. It didn't really matter to him so long as they evened the score for Stoker.

Due to retrieving the buggy with Jeff, it was the following day before Cully was ready to leave the Melbourne place. He had packed his things in his saddlebags and the single war bag he used for his clothes and rounded up his horse. He had everything strapped onto Ginger's back before he heard the sound of footsteps. He looked over his shoulder to see Victoria, treading carefully on her blistered feet.

"Does Martha know you're out here, Sparks?" he asked, rotating to look at her.

Victoria wore a plain housedress, and her rich, satin-like hair lay over her shoulders. Redness from sunburn tinted her otherwise unblemished face—added evidence of their long trek. To Cully, she had never looked more beautiful.

"I-I tried to talk to Mother, to change her mind, but . . ."

"Yeah, Jeff told me how it was. I don't blame her for wanting to be rid of me. I shouldn't have kissed you."

"No, you shouldn't," she agreed. "You've always been a gentleman—a pain to be around, but a gentleman. Why did you do it?"

"Couldn't help myself, Sparks," he confessed. "I've told myself a thousand times you were too good for me, that I was fortunate to live on the same piece of earth. But my heart kind of shoved my brain aside, and I did what it told me to do."

"That's a pretty lame excuse, blaming your heart for overruling your head."

He grinned. "All right, then, it's something I wanted to do since the first day I set eyes on you. I had the chance, you were vulnerable, so I took advantage of the situation. Is that better?"

"It sounds more like the truth."

"And you, Sparks." He studied her with an intense gaze. "Why did you *let* me kiss you without putting up the slightest bit of resistance?"

She hesitated, as if wanting to deny his assertion, yet

she did not contradict him. "Maybe I was curious," she admitted timorously. "You tell so many wild stories and lies about who you are and where you came from. Maybe I thought a kiss would allow me to discern who and what you are."

"And did you find out?"

Her lips rose at the corners. "Yes, you're exactly what you claimed to be: a rogue, a scoundrel, a drifter who would say or do anything to take advantage of a lady in distress."

He nodded his agreement. "Everything you could want in a man . . . other than wealth or status." His expression clouded, and he grew serious. "Don't marry someone you don't love, Sparks. Life is too short to spend it with a man like Winston. Find yourself someone who will love and cherish you because of who you really are, not because of what you're worth or how good you would look alongside a guy trying to win an election."

"We could lose the ranch," she said quietly. "It's for the good of my family."

"Jeff doesn't want you to sacrifice your future for the sake of a mortgage," he argued. "Make your own choice, and have a life for yourself."

Victoria did not reply to his advice. She lifted a hand and backed away. "Good-bye, Cullen. I wish you luck."

"So long, Sparks. I wish you a plethora of happiness." At her surprised look, he grinned. "Bet you didn't know I had that word in my vocabulary."

"Impressive," she replied. "You never cease to amaze me."

"Wish I could stick around and do more than amaze you," he said seriously. "But I suspect your mother will be along with a scattergun if I linger too long."

As Victoria had already said good-bye, she turned and walked, tender-footed, back toward the house. Cully spied Jeff just inside the door, obviously stationed there to keep Martha from either seeing or preventing Victoria from saying her farewell.

Mounting up on Ginger, Cully waited until the girl was in the house before he put the big mare into motion. The ache in his chest felt as if someone had flattened his heart with a sixteen-pound hammer. He knew he was leaving something behind, something priceless and irreplaceable.

Winston endured his father's glare without flinching. He had stayed out drinking and pining over his future, coming home too late to wake up in time to help open the bank. Standing in his father's office, he knew the man was sorely losing patience.

"Responsibility is what defines a man," Malcolm began the lecture. "If you allow your vices to control your life, you will achieve nothing, be nothing! I want you to feel the pride of accomplishment, know the meaning of purpose, and walk tall among men. Your mother was not perfect, but she had a great sense of decorum and knew how to utilize the social graces. We gave you private tutors and sent you to college to gain knowledge and maturity."

Malcolm visibly set his teeth, battling to contain his

rancor. "And what do you give us in return? What is our thanks for seeing that you have every benefit money can offer?" He snorted his contempt. "You drink hard liquor and chase around with a bunch of shiftless, inebriated cohorts half the night! You mingle with women from the saloons or from side-street alleys, while you have the most beautiful woman in the county waiting to be your bride. You dally away your time and discard money as if it grew on trees." He paused to take a breath. "Yes, I've noticed the rather large withdrawals you've been making lately." He tossed up his hands as if giving up all hope. "Damn it all, Winston, you can't even get to work on time—not for the two days of the week you are to help here at the bank.

"What's the matter with you? What are you thinking? Do you want to end up a beggar on the streets, a drunken bum? Do you like having people say you aren't worth the pain of the woman who gave you birth?"

"What I want, Father," Winston said at last, "is to have a say in my future. You expect me to be someone special—a mayor, a congressman, or a governor—but what about me? What if I don't want those things?"

"And what would be your chosen profession—a drifter or wandering salesman, or perhaps you could find work at some foul-smelling saloon as a bartender? Is your aspiration to be a gambler and sit up all night drinking rotgut whiskey and playing cards? Tell me, Winston, what do you want?"

"I want to choose my own wife," Winston said with some passion. "The girl I've been seeing is not from the saloon or some alleyway; she is respectable and a lady. And I don't have to marry Victoria Melbourne to achieve success as a politician. I can win the job of mayor without her at my side."

Malcolm dismissed his logic. "The papers have been drawn up and are awaiting signatures, Winston. Upon your wedding, our ranch is going to merge with the Melbourne place. With the bank and the largest cattle spread in Wyoming, we will control this entire part of the country."

"You're already getting the Sanson ranch, along with his cattle, for practically nothing. Isn't that enough? Why do I have to marry someone just to increase your wealth?"

"Financial savvy is something you never learned, not even with all of the expensive tutors and instructors I provided for you."

"I know enough to get by."

Malcolm groaned. "That's all you want out of life isn't it? To get by! You've no ambition, no determination, not a drop of zest for success or achievement. You're so damned worthless, I'll be forced to spend a fortune to try to get you elected as a lowly town mayor!"

"And you always demand a sizable return on your investment, don't you, Father?" Winston fought back. "I'm forced into a marriage so you can gain control of every ranch in this valley. You claim I have no ambition, but your lust for power knows no bounds. You'll never be satisfied with me, no matter what I do!"

"Try being a man," Malcolm sneered. "I would settle for that much."

Winston had taken all he could stand. He whirled about and marched out of the office. His eyes burned from lack of sleep, and he had a dull ache at the back of his skull from too much drink the previous night. Everything about his life was rotten.

His mother had been a social enthusiast, eager to buy and wear the latest fashions, hairstyles, and every other obsession she had gotten from gossip or one of the upper social class magazines. She was so full of pretense, he didn't really know what her real personality was—perhaps she hadn't even had one.

When she died, he had not lost a mother, only a familiar face that could be seen going to or coming from the house, always in a hurry and always as decked out as a wedding cake. He could not recall her ever mothering him, not even a hug or kiss good-night. She was the woman who had brought him into the world, but she had never been his mother. There were nannies and maids for that sort of thing.

Father says to marry Victoria, he thought sourly, *but I don't want her for my wife. I want Sandra!*

Winston exited the bank and started toward the saloon, but it was closed at that early hour. He would have to settle for breakfast someplace where he could brood and ponder his fate. A bowl of grits would be appropriate this morning, as he had always hated the tasteless gruel.

Chapter Nine

Ginger was a lively horse, usually alert as a spooked deer, yet she didn't shy away from a gunshot or sudden toss of a rope. Many horses, even well-trained and seasoned ones, balked or danced about if a man fired a shot from their back. A good many would veer off or side-step when the rider used a rope and swung it over his head. But Cully had owned Ginger for five years, since she was a two-year old mare. With the exception of the one time she had been with foal, he'd never wanted his saddle on another horse.

As he approached Elk City, Cully automatically removed the thong from the hammer of his gun. Old habits from the past were still with him, yet he had ridden into an ambush when on the trail with Victoria. Being so careless could have cost a lot more than the death of her favorite horse, Mrs. Butters.

Although he could not imagine who wanted him dead or why, he could not afford to be caught unaware a second time. And that meant expecting trouble at every turn. Looking ahead, he saw a bend in the road, where the dusty and weather-rutted lane made a turn between a rocky projection of boulders and a small hill. There was a slight gully that crossed the trail, due to runoff from melting snow or downpours of rain. A trace of dampness was all that remained from the heavy showers several days back; the trickle of water had pretty much dried up. The ditch caused wagons to proceed with care, and a horse would often slow to make the crossing. If a man was to pick a good spot for an ambush . . .

Ginger's ears perked, and she looked suddenly to one side. Cully caught the fleeting movement out of the corner of his eye. He ducked and dug his heels into Ginger's sides at the same time. She jumped forward, lunging over the natural trench, while he pulled his gun and ducked low in the saddle, ready for a fight.

The gunshot sounded, but the bullet sailed over his head. Cully whirled his mount around and caught sight of the two men. They both had to move in order to draw a bead on him, so he kept Ginger jumping left and right, jerking the reins with his left hand.

A second shot whisked by his ear, and Cully fired back. Both men were shooting wildly now—no aiming, in a panic, as their ambush had become a deadly gunfight.

Cully got off a good second shot, and one of the men doubled over. An instant later, Cully was stung by a bullet from the other man's gun. It caused a sudden streak of pain along his ribs, but he ignored it long enough to take aim.

He caught the second man in his sights—the man's

eyes were wide with foreboding, and a naked fear blanched his face. Cully aimed as the man spun about to run. The bullet smacked the attacker near the center of his back. He was propelled forward from the impact and sprawled onto his face.

Using a steady hand, Cully pulled the reins straight back and brought Ginger to a stop. The mare stood completely still, ready to bolt at the faintest touch of reins or heels to her sides. For a long few seconds, Cully kept the two men covered, ready to shoot if either made a move to lift his gun. The one lying facedown was still, but the one he shot first had folded at the middle and remained on his knees. Warily, Cully stepped down from his horse, ground-reined Ginger, and moved toward the pair.

The mortally wounded man was hunched over, basically sitting on his heels, sucking air in ragged gasps. His gun lay useless on the ground, and he had both hands over his chest. As Cully closed the distance between them, the man lifted his head.

"D-Didn't say nuthin' 'bout you 'speckin' an . . . ambush." He coughed and paused to spit out some blood.

"Why did you try to bushwhack me?" Cully demanded to know. "Who sent you?"

The man glowered up at him, his eyes red, filled with hate and pain. His teeth were clenched against the agony of his wound and the knowledge that he was dying. It appeared he might speak, but he lost the battle with death. His features went slack, the light of life vanished from his eyes, and he spilled onto his back.

Cully holstered his gun and checked the second ambusher. They were both dead. He was in the process of searching the pair when a rider came up the trail. Cully had only spoken to the man once, but he recognized the sheriff. Weathers rode at a lope until he reached the gully; then he pulled back on the reins and stopped, his hand resting on his gun, as he was obviously uncertain what was happening.

"These two jaspers tried to waylay me," Cully told him, keeping his hand away from his gun. I was looking for any kind of identity papers they might have on them."

"Appears they about got the job done," the sheriff replied, taking note of the red stain on Cully's right side.

Reaching down, Cully pulled up his shirt enough to inspect the narrow gash. It was more a scrape than a bullet wound, but it had bled some.

"Only a crease," he told the sheriff. "My horse warned me of the trap in time for me to escape getting shot full of holes."

"You're one of Melbourne's hands, aren't you?"

"Cullen Lomax," he said, "but I no longer work for Jeff. Had a run-in with the real boss of the ranch—his wife. She kicked me off the place."

In spite of the dire situation, complete with a wounded man and two dead bodies, the sheriff laughed. "Martha has always been a spitfire. Few who cross her path walk away unscathed." He climbed down from his horse. "Sheriff Roy Weathers," he introduced himself. "I don't believe we've ever met."

"You know either of these gents, Sheriff?"

Roy stepped over the ditch and joined Cully among the boulders. He took a moment to turn each man's head and take a close look.

"Don't recollect seeing either of them before." He eyed Cully. "Why were they gunning for you?"

"Wish I knew, Sheriff." He explained about the first ambush and the man he had killed out on the trail. "Two attempts to kill me, and I have no idea why."

"Jeff told me you might be willing to lend a hand on the murder of Don Sanson."

"It might not be safe to have me around, Sheriff. Someone is sure enough out to get me."

"I'll take my chances," Roy replied. "Let's find these jokers' mounts, load them up, and head for town. You can get checked out by the doc, and then we'll try to figure out where these two yahoos came from."

It took a few minutes to round up the two men's horses, then secure their bodies over the animals' backs. When they had finished the grisly chore, Cully walked to his still ground-reined horse, standing right where he had left her. He paused to pat her on the neck and tell her what a good girl she was.

"You always so affectionate with your horse?" Roy asked, humor laced into his husky voice. "A man over-hearing you might think you'd been spending too much time herding cattle."

Cully climbed aboard and grinned. "It's like I told you, this little mare warned me of the attack, then helped me dodge bullets while I shot those two bushwhackers from her back. I think that deserves a pat on the head and a few kind words."

"Sounds like a right fine horse." Roy showed a new respect for the animal. "You wouldn't be interested in selling her, would you?"

"Not in this lifetime, Sheriff." He chuckled. "Of course, if I don't figure out why people keep setting up ambushes for me, it might not be all that long of a wait."

Victoria was busy washing clothes when the rider entered the yard. She looked out the window and recognized Chad "Buckles" Bonner, her father's ramrod. His horse was lathered from a hard ride, and he had an anxious look on his face.

Jeff must have heard him arrive as well, because he hobbled to the door and met him before he had time to dismount.

"You'd best have a good excuse for abusing your horse that way," Jeff greeted his foreman. "What's the big hurry?"

"I was at the mercantile in town—it being Friday and our usual day for ordering supplies—when I seen the sheriff taking two bodies over to the undertaker. A couple minutes later, some guy came into the store and said the two dead men had ambushed Cullen Lomax at the dry wash just outside of town. He said Cullen had been wounded but managed to kill both of his attackers."

Victoria tossed the wet garment back into the washtub and flew to the door. She nearly knocked Jeff off of his feet, getting outside where she could see Buckles clearly. He was on the ground, still holding the reins of his horse.

"Cullen was wounded? How bad is it?" she wanted to know. "Did you see him? Did they take him over to the doctor's place?"

"I don't know anything more, Missy," Buckles replied, taking a backward step to ward off the barrage of questions. "That's as much talk as there was betwixt the two of them. I settled up the tally and lit out to bring word out here. It sure sounds like someone wants Lomax under six feet of dirt."

"Saddle me a horse!" Victoria ordered Buckles. "Do it now!"

The foreman hesitated, surprised by her staunch command. Before Jeff could say a word one way or the other, Victoria shouted a second time. "I said *now,* Buckles!"

"Yes, ma'am," he replied smartly. Whirling about, he led his horse and jogged toward the barn and corral.

"You don't have to go to town." Jeff tried to calm her. "I'll send one of the boys to check on Cully."

"The man saved my life, Father," she told him firmly. "I'm not going to sit here for the next two or three hours and wonder if he is hurt and maybe dying."

"I won't have you riding alone, not after the attack on you and Cully."

Victoria stared at him with a determined gaze. "I'm going, Daddy, and that's all there is to it!"

She didn't listen for his response but hurried to get changed into her riding dress and boots. By the time she returned to the yard, Martha was standing alongside her husband. There was a hard set to her jaw, but Jeff had obviously dissuaded her from trying to stop Victoria from making the ride. It took but a moment to understand why.

Buckles led two horses from the barn, one saddled for Victoria and the other for himself.

"Until we know what's going on, it's best if you don't ride alone," Jeff told her carefully. "Buckles will see that you get there and back safely."

Rather than spurn his decision, Victoria was relieved he had accepted that she was going without more of a fight—especially with her mother's irate glare displaying proof of her disapproval.

"Thank you, Daddy." She tried to project a gracious air. "I'll be back as soon as I can."

Buckles mounted up on his horse and waited for Victoria to get astride her mount. Then the two of them were pounding the trail at a gallop, heading for town.

Concho kept his distance but saw that Cullen Lomax was not seriously hurt. His two hired men, on the other hand, would be a scourge to the Territory no more. They had failed to do the simple chore given them.

That damn good-for-nothing handyman! What is he, one of God's favorite children? He cursed and kicked a nearby can, sending it flying some twenty feet. Quickly, he reversed his direction and cut into an alley. It wasn't smart to draw attention to himself. He lived a dangerous existence, where one mistake could mean his death.

He had to remain in control of his emotions and figure a new way to be rid of Cullen Lomax.

This whole thing had gone askew. After offing Don Sanson, the second job had sounded sweet, like easy money—just tend to the early demise of a certain troublesome person, and ride out. But Lomax had proven he was not an easy man to kill. He had somehow sniffed out their ambush on the trail, killed Stoker, and nicked him in the arm too. Now he had managed to walk away from a second deadly attack. The man definitely had Lady Luck camped on his shoulder.

Concho mulled over ideas and plans, seeking to sort out one sure way to kill the nuisance handyman. If he knew the man's weakness, he might be able to use it against him. Obviously a careful man, it would take something special to prod Lomax into a mistake. But what could he use to gain an advantage? What did the man care about enough to risk or sacrifice his own life for?

Concho exited the passageway and walked along the rear of several buildings, before he returned by way of a different alley. He decided to watch and see if Lomax appeared with a bandaged arm or something. If his gun hand or that side of his body was injured, it might leave him vulnerable. After witnessing the man in action, and considering he'd killed Stoker, Gunther, and Finn, Concho wanted an enormous edge before making a third attempt to kill him.

He stopped suddenly just before he reached the main street as a man crossed his path, not fifteen feet away.

Concho heard the fellow call someone over who had just arrived on a horse. He quickly ducked out of sight, pressing up against the wall of the building. A moment passed, and a rider stopped a few feet from the alley. A quick peek was enough for him to recognize the girl from the wagon. Victoria Melbourne.

"I rode out to speak with you the other day, Victoria, but you were over visiting your brother." Winston Vanderpool spoke up. "What are you doing in town?"

She sounded out of breath. "There was a gunfight a short while ago. Someone said our handyman, Cullen Lomax, was shot."

"He looked fine to me," Winston replied. "I saw him enter the jail with the sheriff not five minutes ago. They brought in two bodies—men your handyman killed."

"They ambushed him back up the trail a short piece." Another man spoke up.

"Yes, Buckles, I've heard the story . . . as it was told by the only survivor of the fight."

Victoria's voice was immediately defensive and harsh. "What are you insinuating, Winston?"

"I didn't mean anything," Winston backpedaled. "I'm just saying, we got news Lomax had killed another man a couple of days back. It seems to me as if the man is killing a lot of people lately."

"He was protecting *me* when he killed the other man, Winston. Those murdering vermin killed Mrs. Butters. They would have killed us both!"

"Mrs. Butters?" he repeated blankly. "Oh, your favorite horse."

"I'm sorry." Victoria's tone was impatient. "Did you want to speak to me about something?"

"Yes, but not out here on the street, in front of your hired help and the entire town."

"Well, I'm going to check on Cullen. If you wish, we can speak after I see for myself that he is all right."

Winston sounded unhappy to be put off. "When I ran into you at the mercantile earlier this morning, Buckles, I thought you said the handyman had been fired."

"Mother is the one who fired him," Victoria countered. "And it doesn't mean I'm not concerned about his welfare."

"You seem a trifle *overly* concerned to me . . . especially considering he no longer works for you."

Concho snickered to himself and began to back slowly down the alley. He hoped Winston Vanderpool had clean feet, because he had just stuck one or both squarely into his own mouth. Even as he slipped away, Concho heard Victoria shredding Winston's hide with some choice and not so ladylike words. However, the encounter had told him what he needed to know, and it gave him a direction in which to proceed. It was time to change tactics.

Cully was shirtless when the door to the sheriff's office was suddenly opened. He and Roy both swung about to see Victoria framed in the entranceway. She took a single step into the room, saw that Cully was in a state of undress, and froze in midmotion.

"Cully . . . uh, Sheriff . . ." she stammered inanely. "I wanted . . . I was . . . ."

"Come in, Miss Melbourne," Roy invited. "Lomax here was just changing out of his bloody clothes. I'm sure you've seen a man without his shirt on before."

Cully grinned. "I believe she's seen *me* like this a time or two when I was chopping wood out at her ranch."

"I was . . ." She cleared her throat. "I was concerned when I heard you had been wounded."

"More a scratch than an actual wound." Cully dismissed her concern. "The bandage"—he indicated the cloth wrapped about his upper waist—"is only to protect the graze until it heals."

"Oh," Victoria murmured weakly. She lowered her eyes to hide her feelings, but a healthy flush colored her cheeks. "I-I'm glad you're all right."

"I'm as proud as a peacock that you would ride all this way to see that I wasn't seriously wounded, Sparks."

"Yes, well, I had to come into town anyway." She took a step back onto the porch. "If you'll excuse me, I really must be going."

"Thanks for checking on me," Cully said. "It means a lot."

The girl said a stiff good-bye while still refusing to make eye contact and quickly closed the door.

Cully stared after her, wishing he had the courage to follow. He had no idea what he could say or do, but he hated to let her walk away.

"You have a look on your face like someone stole that favorite roan horse of yours," Roy said. "Me not being an actual trained detective, I could pretend I don't know what that means."

"Can you blame me?" Cully asked. "Victoria is the sweetest gal in the county."

"She showed a measure of worry about your welfare too, Lomax. What are you going to do about it?"

Cully uttered a sigh as he tucked in his clean shirt. "She's like a full moon, Roy, bright and beautiful but well beyond the reach of an ordinary man like me."

"I know exactly what you mean, son. Once upon a time I had a hankering for her mother, Martha, but Jefford Melbourne was the son of a businessman. He knew how to bump shoulders with the social crowds and was on equal footing with a wealthy rancher's daughter."

"It sounds as if you and I have a few things in common."

"The truth is," Roy said, "when I left to find some adventure, Martha was too young to court. By the time I got back, it was too late. I never had the chance to tell her how I felt about her, so I'll never know if she would have picked me over Jeff. You still have that option—a chance to compete for Victoria's hand. If you don't at least try, I'll tell you certain, you'll regret it for the rest of your life."

"What you say makes sense, Roy," Cully allowed, "but only if I'm alive to make the effort. We need to solve Don's murder and figure out who wants me dead."

"Any way in hell the two things could be related?"

"I can't see how. I only met Don a time or two and never spent any time with the men on his spread. That rules out my knowing something special or secretive about him or his ranch."

"Let's stick to you, then. Jeff told me about your past. Any way this can be someone trying to get even with you?"

"I left that world behind and was known by an assumed name," Cully said. "And, besides all that, there's something else that make no sense."

"Such as?"

"When Miss Melbourne and I were ambushed, the first shot was to kill our horse." Roy's puzzled expression told Cully he didn't know what that meant. "Why stop the buggy in such a way, unless you intend to kill both passengers?"

"Maybe it was to disable you and leave you stranded."

"That's possible, but a carriage isn't going to make good time over the uneven terrain anyway. Had the pair intended a holdup, they would have had a full day's head start on us by the time we could have reported the robbery."

"You can't be thinking those two planned on killing Victoria too?"

"I don't know, Roy. They came from the Elk City side and waited for us. What I can't figure is how they knew I was with Victoria and would be on that trail."

"Well, this second attack proves they were sure enough after you. So maybe killing the horse on the first try was because they didn't want any witnesses, or it might have been their intention to strand Victoria miles from any help. Disabling the carriage also allowed them to shoot her if she saw their faces. That way they could prevent anyone from knowing who committed the crime."

"Those are possibilities, Roy. Let's hope someone recognizes one of our dead bushwhackers. It would give us a direction to follow."

"The undertaker is going to place them for viewing this afternoon. I asked him to post a sign so as many people as possible will have a look."

"Meanwhile, do you have any thoughts on Don Sanson's death?"

"Every direction I go is a box canyon," Roy said. "I can't figure the why or who of his murder.

"Jeff told me you had talked to a good many people. Tell me what you've learned."

Roy outlined what had taken place from the time he was notified about the killing. He gave a thorough account of his actions and what he had picked up from interviews and conversations. He finished by telling him about Zeke Pullman's being appointed to take over the Sanson ranch.

"I never met up with Pullman, but then, I don't know a good many of the ranch hands from Malcolm Vanderpool's spread."

"If a man were to look at this from a purely financial standpoint, it would seem that Malcolm is going to get himself a ranch, one with major access to water, for the mere price of the loan he made to Sanson."

"I remember Jeff's telling me that Malcolm approached both him and Don about buying some of their range. He wanted access to water for his beef without their mixing with another herd or having to go a couple of miles downstream."

"Yes, and the cattle sickness never touched his spread. That could be coincidental or just plain convenient for Malcolm, but it is on the suspicious side."

"This sickness—it was what is known as the Texas fever?" Cully asked.

The sheriff bobbed his head affirmatively. "Zeke rode out and took a look at the ailing cattle—said he recognized it as the fever. As for myself, I had never seen any infected beef from the old days. But I remember that quarantine laws were passed the year after the war ended back in Eastern Kansas and Western Missouri to keep Texas longhorns out. The ranchers knew the fever was brought in by Texas cattle, but no one ever figured out how it was passed to the local beef."

"You talked to the men on the Vanderpool ranch. Any of them strike you as being cold-blooded enough to gun down Sanson?"

"I haven't gotten around to all of them personally, but the men I've spoken to don't strike me as anything more than cowpunchers. Whoever killed Don was confident and deadly . . . one bullet to the heart."

"Strangers in town?"

"We always have drifters coming through, plus the stage, and we're on the main trail for those who don't take the train running east and west. I'd guess there are a dozen new faces in town at any given time."

Cully thought for a moment. "The obvious motive

for killing Don would be to acquire his ranch. That points the finger of suspicion at Malcolm or Winston Vanderpool."

"Winston isn't crazy about the upcoming wedding, but he's a browbeaten young man who hasn't learned how to stand up to his father. I don't know that he would try anything without Malcolm's say-so."

"Unless it's to prove himself a man," Cully said.

"I guess that's possible," the sheriff answered. "Besides, everyone knows that Winston's been seeing another woman regularly. If Malcolm gains control of Don's ranch, it ought to remove the necessity of Winston's marrying Victoria."

"I think the first thing we need to find out is who was behind the Texas fever from last year. If it was a small herd passing by, there will be people up the trail who know about it. If someone intentionally infected those beef, it might be the key to Don's murder." Cully made the summation. "And you said the man who recognized Texas fever—this Zeke Pullman character—works for Malcolm Vanderpool?"

"Zeke Pullman, yes," Roy told him. "He said he'd seen the fever before, and, when I spoke to him out at Don's ranch, he mentioned that he had trailed herds from Texas and had ridden for Goodnight."

"Charles Goodnight of the Goodnight Trail?"

"The very same. I remember hearing of how he had armed guards who rode his range to keep Texas longhorns from getting near his own beef. He knew they carried the fever."

"So Pullman had some dealings with Texas fever." It was a statement.

"He admitted as much," Roy said. "And he hired on with Malcolm shortly before the fever hit Don and Jeff's cattle."

Cully and Roy looked at each other, both on the same train of thought. Cully put it into words.

"Zeke Pullman brought in the fever!"

Chapter Ten

Victoria had been embarrassed by the encounter at the jail, but she didn't wish to leave town without speaking to Cully in private. She wanted to talk to him, to tell him . . . what? She didn't know. She had returned to her horse and crossed the street, not wanting to appear desperate over the man or stricken like a lovesick schoolgirl. But now she was at a loss as to what to do.

"Want me to water the horses before we return home?" Buckles asked, breaking into her silent tomb of bewilderment.

"Yes, go ahead," she replied. "And then you can have a drink at the saloon or whatever you want for a bit. I've got to speak to Winston and . . ." She didn't finish with an explanation, saying only, "I might be a little while."

"Okay, I'll meet you at the livery in—what, an hour?"

"That ought to be about right."

Buckles took the reins of both horses and started toward the livery. Victoria waited until he had reached the barn before taking a last look at the jail. Cully and Roy were still together, so she headed for the bank. Winston would be sitting at a desk or speaking to customers, but she knew he would make time to talk privately. After all, she was the woman he was going to marry.

Victoria groaned inwardly at the prospect. She didn't want to marry Winston. Visiting her brother and having been around Cully the past few days had convinced her that she wanted a man she could love. She had no desire to be wed to a social figurehead or man of title, paraded about for show or forced to live a life of pretension. With a determined resolve, she made the decision. She was going to tell Winston to his face that she could not go through with the arranged marriage. If that meant having his father foreclose on their ranch, she would make it known throughout all of Elk City that she had been forced into a marriage pact to save their ranch. That wouldn't set well with the voters. Her speaking out could cost Winston the election and any future positions of prominence, the one thing Malcolm Vanderpool so adamantly desired for his son.

She felt better having a plan, even though it meant butting heads with her mother. Martha would rant and scream—she would call Victoria ungrateful and disloyal to the family—but she felt her father would take her side. She knew he was not happy about allowing her to sacrifice her future for the sake of their ranch. He would find an alternate way to save the ranch and Avery's inn without bartering his only daughter. This would work. She would soon be free of—

A brutal hand clamped over Victoria's mouth. Before

she could get her mind to function, she had been dragged into an alleyway, and a knife blade was against her throat.

"Cry out, and I'll slice your throat from ear to ear," an iniquitous voice hissed.

The attacker slowly removed his hand from her mouth and took hold of her shoulder. His fingers dug into the flesh, while the blade of the knife remained pressed to her throat. She dared not turn her head and try to see his face.

"Come along quietly," he whispered harshly. "You're worth nothing to me dead, but that doesn't mean I won't slit your throat."

"W-What do you want with me?" Victoria asked timidly.

"We're going to take a little ride," the man replied. "You cooperate, and you won't be harmed. I'm only looking to make a few bucks."

"But my family is in financial trouble," she informed him. "We don't have enough cattle going to market to even pay the mortgage; we are broke."

"I'll worry about how I get the money, sweetheart. You just walk quietly ahead of me to the back of the tanner's shop. I've got two horses waiting."

Victoria had no choice. When they reached the rear of the building, the man bound her hands behind her and put a blindfold over her eyes. She was led a short way until they reached the place where he had horses waiting. He was a strong man, because he was able to lift her up onto the back of a horse. After taking a moment to shorten the stirrups and see that she was settled, the man got aboard his own horse. Victoria's mount began to move, and she knew she was being led away from town.

As she rocked with the horse's motion, Victoria's mind was sucked into a whirlwind of fear and apprehension. She had no idea who her captor was or where he was taking her. Terror gripped her at the stark realization: *I've been kidnapped!*

Cully and Roy Weathers were discussing the best way to go forward with what they had learned. Zeke Pullman would have to confess to the fever scheme but also implicate Malcolm Vanderpool. And there was still the murder of Don Sanson to consider. Malcolm could have ordered the shooting, but he was already set to get half of the Melbourne spread. Why risk something so dangerous?

Concerning an alternate problem, who was trying to kill Cully and why?

Before they had outlined a battle plan, the door burst open, and Buckles Bonner came rushing in. He had a piece of paper in his hand.

"I just found this note pinned to the wall in the alley next to the bank!" he declared, his tanned features blanched with fear. "And I've looked all over town—she's gone!"

Roy stepped over, took the note, and read it. "It's a ransom demand," he said solemnly, "for Victoria Melbourne."

"What?" Cully was stunned. "Someone grabbed Victoria?"

Roy showed him the piece of paper. "The kidnapper wants five thousand dollars." He spoke as Cully examined the writing. "And he wants *you* to deliver the money."

Cully swore an oath but resisted the temptation to crush the paper in his hands. Rage was a lethal emotion that often got people killed. He needed his wits about him.

"Come alone." He read the message aloud. "Bring the money, and ride to the rock face of Boulder Point. Be there at noon tomorrow. There will be directions to follow from there."

"Smart," Roy said. "Boulder Point is miles away from any real cover. The kidnapper will be able to see if anyone is with you or follows."

"And he can send me to another two or three locations for instructions, so he can make sure I'm alone," Cully agreed.

"This could be a trap to get to *you*," Roy pointed out. "Someone has tried to kill you twice, and this insures you will be by yourself."

Cully dismissed the warning. "Where do we get the five thousand dollars? The Melbourne place is in debt up to their ears, and the cattle drive is weeks away."

"Gotta be Vanderpool," Buckles offered. "Malcolm's son is supposed to marry Victoria. I'll bet he'll put up the money to get her back."

Cully wanted to jump onto a horse and ride out, try to catch the kidnapper before he reached Boulder Point, but he knew that the man would be watching his own trail. This was Victoria; he had to first get the money and then follow the instructions. He couldn't risk Victoria's being hurt, even if it cost him his life.

Roy slumped into a chair and groaned. "I'm ready to turn in my badge. This whole situation gets worse every damn day. Cattle dying by the hundreds last year, Don Sanson killed, two attempts on your life, and now a kidnapping. Holy hell, Lomax, I wasn't cut out for this!"

"Don't quit the game before we get our turn, Sheriff," Cully told him in a firm tone of voice. "I'd be willing to bet we are on the right track concerning Don Sanson's death. As for this kidnapping, it doesn't matter if it's for the ransom or if I'm the target; I'll soon get the answer to that too."

"If you go out there alone, whoever is trying to kill you will have the perfect opportunity to get the job done—and collect five thousand dollars for his trouble!"

Cully didn't argue but turned to the business at hand. "You need to take this ransom note to the bank and see about getting the money. I've got to head down to the livery and have a word with the blacksmith. I'll meet you back here in a little while."

Buckles shook his head. "I think the sheriff is right, Cullen. This could be a trick to kill you. They tried twice before. This time, you'll be following directions, out there as naked and exposed as a wart on the end of a fellow's nose!"

"If it's me the kidnapper wants, he'll have his chance."

"You ain't bulletproof, Lomax," Roy reminded him. "Soon as you hand over the money, that jasper can shoot you dead."

"Speak to Malcolm, and get me the five thousand," Cully told the sheriff. "If things work out, he ought to have his money back in a day or two."

Buckles snorted. "Got to admire his attitude, don't you, Sheriff? Anyone would think he's the one who has all the chips in this here game."

Roy took the note and sighed. "I'll talk to Malcolm and get together the money somehow. You sound so all-fired confident, I'll back your play . . . leastways until you end up as buzzard bait."

As the sheriff left the office, Cully looked at Buckles. "You'd better ride out and tell Jeff what has happened. Be sure you let him know that we're going to do whatever it takes to get his girl back safely."

"You got it, Cullen," the hired hand answered. He paused before leaving. "And if it's any consolation, me and the other boys don't think it was right for Mrs. Melbourne to fire you. Whatever was going on betwixt you and Victoria . . . well, we figure you for a decent and honorable sort."

"Trust me when I say I would die rather than shame Victoria, Buckles."

The man stuck out his hand. "Good luck to you. Anything you need, just let out a holler. I'll have every man jack from the ranch in town to back your play."

Cully took his hand in a firm shake and then watched him go. He had no time to think about might-have-beens with Victoria. She had come into town to check on his injuries. She had left herself vulnerable because of him. He would not let her down.

Winston Vanderpool followed Roy Weathers into his father's office in the bank. Malcolm bid him to close the door for privacy, then frowned at the sheriff.

"What's so important that it couldn't wait until after dinner?" the banker asked with some impatience. "Does this have to do with Don's murder?"

Roy handed the ransom demand to Malcolm. Winston moved around behind his father's desk so he could read over his shoulder.

"Victoria?" Winston's voice squeaked. "She's been kidnapped?"

"This note was left where Buckles Bonner would find it when Victoria didn't show up at the livery. We searched the town and came up empty."

"Where was Victoria supposed to be?" Winston asked.

"She was coming to speak to you, or so she told Bonner."

"Well, she never entered the bank," he replied. "I've been at my desk all day long, except for when you and the Melbourne handyman brought in those two dead men. I would have spoken to her when she rode in, but she was too worried that Lomax had been seriously hurt. I told her the man was all right, but she wasn't inclined to take my word for it. When I left her, she was going over to the jail. I don't know where she went after that."

"Yes," Roy said, "she stopped in for a minute and then left. That's when the lady and Buckles parted company. She told him to meet her at the stable in an hour. When she didn't show, he found this ransom note tacked to the bank wall."

"Five thousand dollars," Malcolm muttered. "That's a lot of money."

"Cullen says he'll get the money back once Victoria is set free."

Malcolm laughed without humor. "That's quite a boast for a handyman."

"I believe him."

"You put a lot of stock in that man, Sheriff. How do we know this isn't his doing?"

"You've got my word," Roy stated firmly. "You can also have the word of Jefford Melbourne if you doubt me."

"All right, all right." He waved a dismissive hand. "I was only thinking how the man seems to be in a lot of trouble lately. Two attempts on his life—what if this is all a ploy to get him out where one of those killers can finish him?"

"It's a possibility, but we won't know unless we can pay the ransom."

"We've got enough cash on hand." Winston jumped into the conversation. "I counted the money this morning for the weekly audit. We've got to pay up, Father."

"First you don't want to marry the girl, and now you

want me to spend a fortune to pay her ransom. I thought it was women who were fickle."

"It's the right thing to do," Winston maintained.

"This kind of thing will look good for your boy here, come election time," Roy put in. "Especially if he should decide not to marry the girl. His forking over the money to see to Victoria's safe return—that'd go a long way with the voters."

Malcolm bobbed his head. "All right," he gave in. "When do you need it?"

"Note says to be at the location at noon tomorrow," Winston pointed out from the wording in the ransom note. "What is it to Boulder Point, Sheriff, about a four-hour ride?"

"Yes, and there's no cover for miles. It won't be possible to try anything."

Malcolm glanced at his son. "Have the money ready first thing in the morning." Diverting his attention to Roy, he said, "We'll pay up and hope your man is good enough to get our money back for us."

Roy met his gaze and returned a stern look. "If he fails, it will only be because he is dead."

Victoria kept her mouth shut and rode blindly for what seemed an endless time. She could feel the heat of the sun, so it was some comfort that she had donned her riding outfit before coming into town. Her captor offered not a word, nor even a sip of water to ease her parched throat.

Finally, her horse stopped. She sat and waited, but the

man did not speak. She heard him dismount, and there came a rustling as if he was going through his saddle-bags. Next it sounded as if he walked a short distance and returned. After a few minutes they began to move again.

"Tell me about your handyman," her kidnapper ordered. "Where the hell did he learn to shoot like that?"

Victoria tried to speak, but several hours with nothing to drink had left her too dry. She licked her lips and swallowed to moisten her throat before she could get any words out.

"I don't know," she answered hoarsely.

"You must know what the guy did before he came to work for you."

"Cully is a storyteller," she said. "He spins so many tales, you don't know what to believe." She waited, but the man fell silent again. After a few moments she posed a question to him. "You're the one who's been trying to kill him," she pointed out. "You must have a reason for wanting him dead."

"He was supposed to be a regular ranch hand," the man responded. "I don't know anything about him—other than that he killed my partner and two hired men."

"He'll kill you too," she warned him. "You made a big mistake taking me. Cully is a very competent and determined man."

The fellow chuckled. "I thought you were engaged to be married, yet you sound like you admire your handyman more than your husband-to-be."

"Cully will not let you get away with this," she

retorted. "You might want to reconsider this kidnapping and let me go."

"Don't you worry about me, little lady. I'm not going to take any chances with your handyman. A man as good with a gun as he is—nope, I'm not taking any chances at all."

Victoria didn't like the sound of that. However, the man stopped speaking and continued leading her on an unknown journey. She didn't know where they were headed, but she hadn't heard another living being for several hours, not even a cow bawling in the distance. They were obviously headed to someplace solitary, where her kidnapper would be able to see Cully's approach.

Fear gripped her heart, not for herself, but for Cully. He would do as he was told, not daring to put her life at risk. That meant he would follow directions and ride up, exposed and in the open—a perfect target for the kidnapper.

What can I do? she lamented inwardly. *Somehow I must warn him. This kidnapper intends to kill him . . . and probably me as well.*

Winston stood at Sandra's door, but Bud refused to allow him to enter.

"You remember what my sister told you," Bud reminded him. "So long as you're engaged to Miss Melbourne, you're not welcome here."

Winston looked past him, but Sandra had purposely moved from sight. She refused to even see him.

"Listen to me, Bud"—Winston pleaded his case—"everything has changed."

"You said as much when Sanson died. Once your father ended up with the deed to his ranch, the wedding thing was supposed to go away. The thing is, I've not heard a word about anyone calling off the engagement between you and Victoria."

"I would have, but I didn't get the chance!" he cried. "She was out of the valley—she went to visit her brother—and then there was the whole ambush thing. Before I could talk to her, her father's handyman was involved in a second shootout—you probably heard about it. Anyway, I told her I wanted to see her today, but someone kidnapped her, and—."

"What did you say?" Sandra asked, coming from behind the door. "Someone kidnapped Victoria?"

"Yes, this afternoon," he explained. "She told Buckles Bonner that she was coming to talk to me. It's the conversation I've been trying to arrange. I was going to tell her the wedding was off. I swear, Sandra, it's why I wanted to see her! But someone grabbed her and left a ransom note. She's been taken by some kidnapper, and they want Lomax to pay the ransom tomorrow."

Sandra put a hand on her brother's arm, and he moved to allow her to step up and stand before Winston. "I hadn't heard about any kidnapping. No one said anything at the store."

"The news hasn't had time to spread. I spent the last hour or so getting together the money at the bank."

Sandra didn't hide her surprise. "*You* are paying the ransom?"

Winston lifted his shoulders in a helpless gesture. "Who else is there? The Melbourne ranch is up to its neck in debt because of the cattle they lost last year, plus Jefford borrowed money to help his son get started in his own business. They don't have enough credit to buy a good meal in town."

"How much is the kidnapper asking for?" Bud wanted to know.

"Five thousand dollars."

Sandra gasped. "Five *thousand* dollars!"

"Were you able to raise that much money?" Bud was also concerned. "I didn't realize you had that much cash in your bank."

"It took 'most every cent we had on hand." He regarded them both with a solemn look. "Please don't say anything to anyone about the ransom amount or us paying it. If it became known the bank had advanced that much money, some people might think we couldn't repay their savings. If there was a run on the bank, with a huge number of withdrawals, it could cause us a lot of trouble. Father has more money in a bank back east, but he can't get it here for several days."

"Who *is* going to repay the ransom money?" Sandra asked. "I don't see your father as being the softhearted sort to simply give it away."

"The sheriff said Lomax claimed he would get the money back after he secures the safe release of Victoria."

Bud uttered a cynical grunt. "Man don't think much of himself, does he?"

"I agree," Winston said. "I don't see how he can make such a promise, but the sheriff is backing his claim. I guess if the money is lost, we'll add the amount to the Melbourne debt. That would pretty much give us their ranch without the necessity of a wedding."

Sandra did not hide her eagerness. "So you're going to be free of the marriage, regardless of how this turns out?"

"I promised you I wasn't going to marry Victoria, my dearest," Winston said. He reached out and took hold of her hand. "You're the woman I want to spend my life with."

Bud pushed past Winston. "If you two are going to get all cozy like, I'll be leaving." He donned his hat and added solemnly, "I sure hope nothing bad happens to Miss Melbourne or the handyman."

Winston bobbed his head in agreement but waited only until Bud had taken a few steps down the hallway before he took Sandra into his arms. She came willingly this time, and her kiss was warm and sweet.

Cully spent a couple of hours with the blacksmith before calling it a night. He knew he wouldn't be able to sleep, so he stopped by the saloon, found an empty table, and ordered a beer. Sometimes a drink would help him relax. And he needed to try not to think about Victoria and how terrified she might be at that very moment.

"Winston told me about the mess you're in," Bud Longmont said, having arrived carrying two mugs of beer in his hands. "Barkeep told me this one was yours." He indicated one glass and set it down in front of Cully. He plopped down in the chair opposite him and sipped a swallow of his own brew.

"I don't believe you and I ever met face-to-face."

"I've seen you around," Cully said. "You've a pretty kid sister."

That brought a smile to his face. "I've raised her the past dozen years. Ma died when Sandra was eight, and Pa passed away a couple of years later. Been a tough road for her, but she learned to sew and earns enough to get by."

"I've heard you do a little of most everything too." Cully grinned. "I believe there's a job open at the Melbourne ranch for a handyman."

Bud chuckled. "Not for me. Mrs. Melbourne has a nasty reputation, one I don't wish to put to the test."

"She rules the roost, sure enough."

"Thanks anyway, but I'm supposed to start work as a stage driver starting next month. They've got an older gent set to retire, and one of their other drivers hurt his shoulder and can't drive the team. Looks as if it might work out to be the permanent sort of job I've been looking for."

"I wish you luck."

"Don't wish me any of your luck, Lomax. You're the one who's going out to pay the ransom tomorrow."

Cully smiled. "I've been in a jam or two before. I'm hoping to get out of this with a whole skin."

Bud grew pensive and leaned over the table. "I walked by the grave-digger's place and took a look at the two men who jumped you," he said carefully. "I remember seeing a fellow having a conversation with those two jaspers here at the saloon."

Cully was instantly alert. "You did? When?"

"The day before yesterday, I believe it was. The guy talking to them didn't give me cause to think anything was up, but seeing as how them boys tried to kill you . . ."

"What can you tell me about him—the third man, I mean?"

Bud took a long swig of beer and wiped a trace of foam from his mouth. "He arrived in town a couple of weeks back with another fellow . . . big man with a scar on his chin."

"Sounds like the man I killed on the trail a few days back."

"Anyway, I didn't hear much of what was said, but one of the two dead men called him by the handle of *Concho*. That mean anything to you?"

Cully sat up straight at the name. "I've heard of a gent who handles—shall we say, *difficult?*—jobs who goes by that name. Supposed to be a hired killer."

"He isn't much to scare a person on sight: a little bigger than average height and weight, with shaggy brown hair and some poor-looking teeth. Carries a Colt on his right hip and a big skinning knife on his left. Not the kind of guy to cause much attention, but there was a set to his manner and a glint in his eyes, reminded me of a snake ready to strike. I remember thinking how I wouldn't want to be on his bad side."

"Have you seen him since he spoke to those two bushwhackers?"

Bud tipped his glass and emptied it before answering. "I saw him hanging around for a few minutes last night, but I haven't seen him today."

"He could be the one who grabbed Victoria."

"Maybe he's also the guy trying to kill you," Bud remarked. "Any reason someone would hire a man like him to put you in a box?"

"Not that I can think of."

"Well, I don't know if any of this will help, but I thought I ought to tell you. I hope you manage to put that kidnapper in a hole and bring the girl home safely."

"Thanks, Bud. It helps to put a name to the man who has targeted me . . . even if I don't know why."

The young man rose from the table, leaving behind his empty glass. "Be seeing you around"—he gave a grim smirk—"providing you come back."

Cully lifted a hand in farewell and turned to thoughts of the man known as Concho. He recalled seeing a WANTED notice on the man once. The list of charges was extensive, but he had never been caught.

He wondered if kidnapping Victoria had been the intention of the first ambush. Killing the horse would have prevented her escape. If the two men had killed Cully, they could have taken the girl hostage then and there. As for the second attempt on his life, that might have been personal, or perhaps they misunderstood his job on the ranch. If they thought he was Victoria's bodyguard, it would have been necessary to remove him to get to her.

Cully pushed the glass away. He would head over to the jail and take a bunk in a cell. It wasn't as if he would get any sleep, but he could close his eyes and rest his body. Knowing he was dealing with the notorious Concho, he would need to be especially careful and vigilant.

Chapter Eleven

Victoria sat quietly on the saddle blanket, unable to keep her mouth from watering. From what her senses could detect, her captor was frying bacon and warming beans. He had not offered her so much as a sip of water, so she tried to mentally prepare herself in case she was forced to go both hungry and thirsty.

"I got to admit"—the sound of the man's voice caused her to jump—"you're one fine-looking woman. Easy to see why your ma thinks she can swap you for a king's ransom." He laughed. "Guess that's why they'll pay a king's ransom for you too, huh?"

"What if they can't get you your money?" she asked, hoarse from the dryness of her throat.

"That would be a real shame," he replied. "I'm kind of looking forward to retiring for a spell. Five thousand dollars ought to set me up for a few years."

"It would take a ranch hand ten years to earn that much money."

"Yeah, but I don't intend to live like some broken-down cowpoke. I'm going to enjoy the finer things life has to offer."

Victoria fell silent. After a short while, she listened to the man eating, hating the way he smacked his lips. A hog at the trough made less noise, and she suspected he was making more racket than necessary to annoy her.

"You've got some sand in your craw." He spoke up finally. "Most people would have been whining for something to eat or drink by this time."

"I'm not given to whining."

"Tell you what is going to happen," her captor said. She heard him kicking out the fire. "I'm going to untie you and let you remove your blindfold long enough to eat. When you've finished, you will put the blindfold back on, and I will again tie your hands behind your back." He waited, but she did not reply. "This is for your own good," he added. "You get a look at me, and I'll have to kill you. Do you understand what I'm telling you?"

"Yes, I understand."

She sensed movement behind her. Something was placed on the edge of the blanket, and then her hands were untied. She waited a moment, listening to him back away into the darkness, then carefully removed the cloth covering her eyes. Victoria blinked at the blackness of a moonless night, even though her eyes were used to the thick blindfold. She felt around until she found the tin plate.

There was no fork or spoon, so she was forced to use

her fingers to eat. She was thankful that the kidnapper had also placed a canteen at her side. She drank several times and quickly cleaned the pan. When she finished, she wiped her fingers on a fold of her dress and purposely did not turn to either side. When she heard the sound of the man approaching from behind her, she put the blindfold back into place and held her hands behind her.

"You're a good girl," he offered, wrapping the cord about her wrists. "If this little venture goes off without a hitch, you'll be home in your own bed tomorrow night."

He tested to see that the cloth covering was snug over her eyes, then removed her hat and instructed her to lie down.

It was awkward trying to find a comfortable position, as she had to lie on one arm, but Victoria managed to get herself into a horizontal position. A blanket fell over her, and she was covered from her shoulders to her feet.

"You go moving around during the night, and you'll have frost on your whiskers before morning," he warned. "I'll be around keeping watch, but I'm not playing nursemaid for you."

"I appreciate the consideration," she murmured softly. "Thank you."

The man might have paused for a moment, but then Victoria heard soft footsteps, and he was gone. He seemed to move like a shadow, barely disturbing the air. It caused her to worry about what lay ahead. Cully would come for her—she did not doubt that for a moment—but was he riding to his death? This man had been careless when he and his partner ambushed them up on the old trail. He didn't give the impression of being the kind of man to make the same mistake twice. And this time he knew Cully was deadly with a gun. He would be ready.

Unable to think or do anything about her own predicament, Victoria chose the single path open to her. She began to pray.

Shortly after Cully left town, the stage arrived. Roy Weathers was there to meet it and was pleasantly surprised. The lady onboard looked several years younger than he. As she exited the coach, he noticed that she carried a few extra pounds but seemed comfortable with her age and appearance and moved with a natural grace. Her hair was pulled back from her face, and there was a light powder from the dusty trail on her shoulders and sprinkled on her fashionable hat. She met his inquisitive perusal and smiled. The simple act added worth and charm to her already comely features.

"I presume you are Sheriff Weathers?" she said in greeting.

"Mrs. Carmichael." He presented her with his best smile. "It's very good of you to come so promptly."

"Your telegram was quite persuasive."

"I'm sorry I didn't know to contact you sooner."

"It certainly wasn't your fault. And I'm here now."

Roy took his gaze from her long enough to collect her two pieces of luggage.

"I reserved a room for you at the boardinghouse," he informed her. "They provide an evening meal and also toast and supawn—it's actually cornmeal mush—in the mornings. The place is located next to the bathhouse, and it is much quieter than the hotel."

She gave another smile. "I enjoy being in the company of a man who knows how to take charge. My George was like that," she told him. "George was forever worrying about every detail. I found it irksome at times, but we never lacked for planning. Twenty-one years of marriage, and he never missed paying a bill, and me and the kids never wanted for food or shelter."

"Any kids still living at home?"

"No, we had three, but one was taken by the measles. The two girls are both married and working on families of their own."

Roy cast a sidelong glance. "And George?"

"My husband died some years ago—nearly six years, to be exact."

"That's a shame. Sounds like he was a good man."

"I had no complaints," she replied. "Had he survived me, I hope he would have felt comfortable saying the same thing."

"I'm sure he would."

Roy started off toward the boardinghouse, carrying the bags and leading the way. "There's some trouble hereabouts," he warned her, "so I'd like some time to talk to you in private."

"I shall be happy to accommodate you, Sheriff."

He cocked his head to gaze at her. "That's the best offer I've had since I took this job. May I be so bold as to say you are quite a handsome lady?"

Wilma laughed. "You wouldn't be flirting with me, would you, Sheriff?"

He grinned. "I might be so inclined . . . but not until we discuss the situation here in Elk City."

"Will it cause a scandal if you accompany me to my room for this discussion, or should I settle in and meet you later?"

"You're probably tired from the long ride. How about we get together for lunch—say, about noon at the hotel, the one just down the street?" He hurried to add, "They have the best cook in town."

"That sounds like a very nice arrangement."

They had reached the boardinghouse, so Roy took her things to her room and left her to freshen up and relax from the overnight ride on the stage. She had about two hours before their meeting for lunch, and Roy needed to get a few things done as well. He paused at the walk and looked off in the direction of Boulder Point. He wondered if he would ever see Cullen Lomax alive again. The man was capable, and he claimed to have a plan, but he was riding directly into a trap—a trap set by a killer. There was plenty of reason for concern but nothing Roy could do about the situation but wait.

On another front, however, he and Cully had worked out a suitable plan. It was up to him to carry it forward and hope Cully returned alive. Even if the worst should happen, Roy still had a job to do.

Victoria was given only a few sips of water the following morning, before her captor replaced her hat on her head and bound her to a tree. She tried to find a comfortable position, but the bark rubbed against her wrists, and a knot in the trunk dug into her back. She felt something crawl across her shoulder, and it touched her cheek. She shook her head violently, and whatever it was either flew away or fell off.

The morning passed slowly, and she had no idea where the kidnapper was or what he was up to. Sometimes she thought she heard a soft step or the rustle of a leaf, but the man moved as quietly as a ghost. The only positive thing about her situation was the fact that she was sitting down.

As the day progressed, she felt the sun move from her left side to her lap. As it began to heat her right side, her stomach growled in complaint. She had staved off her hunger and thirst by not using any energy except to breathe and think. Even that was no longer working. Her throat had become parched the previous day, and the single meal was long since forgotten . . . at least by her stomach.

Finally there came the approach of footsteps, and she sensed that her captor had moved to stand over her.

"You've been a right decent sort, Miss Melbourne," he said. "I'm going to be sorry to part company with you."

"You're letting me go?" she asked, her voice only a hoarse whisper.

"Not until I have my money, but the worst of the ordeal is over for you."

She didn't know what that meant, but she held her silence while the kidnapper removed the cord that held her to the tree. His hands were abruptly under her arms, and he lifted her to her feet. She almost collapsed, due to her muscles being weak and stiff from the long hours of sitting.

"This way," he said, leading her along by her upper arm.

Victoria walked for some distance before her kidnapper stopped her. For a moment, she thought he was going to take off her blindfold. However, he only removed her hat—to slip a noose over her head.

"What are you . . . ?"

"Don't get to fretting," he told her. "You have to be visible to your handyman. I'm going to have you step up onto a log I have wedged in a tree. Lomax will be able to see that you are safe and unharmed that way."

"I'm perfectly willing to stand still without a noose around my neck," she offered.

"Sorry, but I need for you to look in peril. Man comes in hell-bent on saving a woman's life, he forgets to be careful." Her captor's voice grew cold. "And I want him to come in real close."

"You're going to kill him."

"I'm going to do just that," he freely admitted.

"But why?" she asked. "What did he ever do to you?"

"He killed my partner."

"Only after you attacked us!"

"Up you go," he said, guiding her foot up onto a tree branch, which felt to be a few inches in diameter. Once she put weight on that foot, he lifted her up so she could stand. The rope came tightly around her neck as he removed the slack.

"W-What if I fall?" she queried. "I don't know how long I can balance on this skinny branch."

"That's why the rope is snug," he said cynically. "You slip, it'll hold you up."

"Hold me up!" she protested. "I'll be strangled to death!"

"So don't slip," he warned her.

Victoria felt unsteady; her legs were stiff and not working properly from her hours of sitting. She lacked strength, as she had been given little food and only a few sips of water since being kidnapped. Gamely, she summoned forth her bravado and vowed to tough it out. Cully was coming. He would have a plan. He would save her, the same as he had saved her twice before.

Cully reached Boulder Point shortly before noon. A paper with new directions was out in the open, held in place by a stone. He followed the map for the next two hours before he spied the indicated destination. The area that lay before him was the end of the hunt. He slowed Ginger to a walk, unhooked the thong from the hammer of his pistol, and took a sweep of the area, alert for any movement. There were a number of rock formations, trees, and stands of brush where a man could hide.

He caught sight of Victoria as he neared the deadly-looking cove. It appeared she was standing a couple of feet off of the ground, teetering on a branch or small log that had been placed between a rotted stump and a split in a crooked tree. A rope had been tossed over a branch a few feet above her head, and a noose was around her neck, tied off about the base of the tree. One mis-step, and Victoria would be hanged.

"I'm here with the money!" Cully called out. "Turn the girl loose, and I'll bring it to you."

"You'd best come a little closer," a voice replied, sounding as if the man were directly ahead. "And don't you dally none, Lomax. The lady ain't all that steady. She falls, and it's farewell to being her hero."

Cully's heart was hammering in his chest, and his breath was short. Sweat beaded his brow and damp-ened his body. Part of the perspiration was due to the jacket he wore. He hoped Concho didn't wonder at his being a bit overdressed for the nearly eighty-degree weather.

"Come on ahead," the man's voice called again. "A few more steps, and I'll cut the girl down. First, I have to make certain you have the money."

"It's in my saddlebags," Cully replied. "Five thou-sand dollars in gold, silver, and paper. We had to clean out the bank to cover the ransom."

"Bet that about caused Vanderpool apoplexy," Con-cho said with a laugh. "Would have enjoyed seeing the man's face when he had to hand over so much of his money."

Cully eased his horse forward until a man appeared less than a hundred feet ahead of him. A rifle was aimed right at Cully's chest. He had never seen the man before, other than a glimpse of his back when he'd lit out on his horse after the botched ambush, but he knew who he was.

"You toss the money this way," Concho said. "Once I check to see it's all here, I'll turn the girl loose."

Cully reached back and removed the saddlebags. He gave a hard toss, and the satchel landed twenty feet in front of Concho.

"Lift your hands like you are praising the lord, Lomax. I don't want no tricks."

Cully did so but watched the man's eyes, hoping for a chance to make a grab for his gun. Concho was not the kind to make that mistake. He used his peripheral vision to locate the saddlebags, while his gaze never wavered from Cully. After a few steps, he had the satchel at his feet.

The rifle's muzzle remained steady as the killer squatted on his heels and used his free hand to undo the strap and open the bag. He felt the sack of gold and silver coin, then removed the wad of paper money. Rather than lowering his head or eyes, he lifted the bills high enough that he could see them, while his vision remained directly on Cully.

"Do I have to count it?"

"It's all there—every dollar."

"Fine," Concho said, returning the money to the pouch. "Guess that takes care of the transaction for the girl."

"You said you would let her go," Cully reminded him.

"Oh, she's free to go . . . whenever she gets tired of standing on that limb." Concho sneered. "And you're free to watch!"

"I'm the one you want," Cully replied. "It's me you came after to start with."

Concho laughed and pulled the trigger.

The bullet hit Cully in the middle of the chest. The impact knocked him backward off of Ginger, and he spilled onto the ground. He lay stunned for a moment, trying to draw air into his lungs.

"Hell, Lomax," Concho called out, "I never even heard of you before you killed my partner. Killing you is payback for you shooting Stoker."

Cully could feel the heat of the sun on his face. His senses were scrambled, but he knew time was not on his side. Lifting his head slightly, he was able to see the kidnapper, while he also took hold of the butt of his pistol.

"If you can still hear me, Lomax"—Concho continued talking while throwing the saddlebags over his shoulder—"I'm glad to finally put you out of my misery." He paused to look over at Victoria. "I give your girlfriend maybe fifteen minutes before she loses her balance and hangs herself. What do you think?"

"I think you shouldn't take killing a man for granted."

Concho swung around. Seeing Cully on his feet with

a gun in his hand, his eyes widened with shock. He rapidly worked the lever on his rifle, jacking a fresh round into the chamber. He lifted the barrel to aim.

Cully fired twice, the shots so close together, they caused only a single echo. The first bullet hit Concho in his left shirt pocket, and the second struck him in the middle of the chest. He dropped like a sack of grain, flopping down to a sitting position before he pitched forward, facefirst, to the ground.

Cully started forward when he heard a gasp and a muffled cry of "Cully!"

Victoria had slipped or lost her balance. She was suddenly hanging. Her feet flailed for the branch, but the limb was not in line with her footing.

Cully grabbed up Concho's rifle, took a split second to aim, and pulled the trigger. The bullet did not cut the rope completely in two but weakened it enough that it could not support Victoria's weight. As Cully began to run forward, the rope snapped, and she landed on the ground.

Cully sprinted around rocks and brush, finally reached her side, and slid down next to her on his knees. His fingers worked the noose from her neck, and he yanked it over her head. To his relief, she choked and gasped for air.

"It's all right," he told her. "You're all right."

She was straining to get air into her lungs, but she managed to sit up under her own power, which allowed Cully to remove the blindfold and untie her wrists. As soon as her hands were free, she threw her arms around him.

"I . . . I heard . . ." Her voice was hoarse, and she had to swallow before she could speak. "I heard the man shoot. I thought he had killed you."

"So you immediately decided to commit suicide to join me in the Hereafter—was that what you were thinking?" he teased.

"I slipped!" she battled back, her spunk already recouped. "I haven't had but a sip of water today, and I've been standing on that rotten tree limb for at least an hour."

"Let me get the canteen."

He started to pull away, but she clung to him and looked up into his face. "I heard him shoot you. I can't believe he didn't kill you!"

Cully applied his knuckles to his chest, and there came the sound of a metallic thud. As she watched in awe, he opened his jacket to reveal a thick metal sheet about the size of the door to a potbellied stove.

"See? Just like one of those fairy tales—the knight in armor saves the damsel in distress."

"You haven't saved me yet." She dampened his enthusiasm. "I still might die of thirst or hunger . . . or from listening to more of your lies and exaggerations."

"Ouch!" he complained. "That's not the way it ends in the fairy tales."

She pushed back from him and waved a hand to start him moving. " 'Happily ever after' will have to wait. Where's your canteen?"

Chapter Twelve

Roy found Zeke Pullman at the house. The man smiled a greeting until he saw the cool expression and hard set of Roy's jaw.

"Something wrong, Sheriff?"

"We're going to take a ride to town for a little chat at my office, Zeke. I'm going to ask some pointed questions, and I want straight answers."

Zeke nervously licked his lips. "What's on your mind? Maybe we can settle things here and now."

Roy ignored the offer. "Get your hat."

Zeke did as he was told, while his shoulders sagged like those of a boy who knew he was due a scolding. After he saddled his horse, the two of them made their way to Elk City. They took the back route to the jail, as Roy didn't want anyone getting wind of what was happening until he had all the cards in order.

"I told you how it was," Zeke complained as he was herded into a cell. "Near forty years I've been a cow tender, wrangler, and drover. I've spent more nights on the ground than in a bed. It gets the better of a man when he gets to be our age—you ought to know that."

"How did you do it?" Roy wanted to know. "How did you infect the Sanson and Melbourne cattle with Texas fever? Far as I know, no one has figured out how the disease is passed from longhorn to other beef."

"Them animal-educated fellers ain't as smart as they like to think," Zeke told him. "I used to tan hides for leather chaps—shotguns, some call them down Texas way—and I've also helped slaughter more than a few cattle over the years. It was when I found some tiny bugs on a longhorn hide that I got the notion."

"Bugs?"

"You know—ticks, them little varmints that can make a person sick or even kill them from time to time. Anyway, I'd never seen this kind of tick on a regular beef, so I rounded up an old cow, locked her in a pen, and put some of them ticks on her. Didn't take no time at all before she was down sick with the fever."

"Why didn't you report it to a government official or something?"

"A pat on the back don't spend for shucks," Zeke replied. "I kept it to myself until I come here looking for work. Malcolm had come to the valley late and was looking to find a way to grow. He needed access to the river, but there were two ranchers here ahead of him."

"So you offered to get rid of their herds?"

Zeke waved a hand at that notion. "Not their whole herds—I didn't want to ruin nobody. Malcolm claimed he would pay a fair price for either Sanson's south pasture or the northern part of Melbourne's ranch. Either place would allow his cattle a clear path to water, and he could add to his herd. I chose to infect the beef where the cattle were separated, so as not to have it spread to the entire herds. It worked out pretty well. After the sickness began to strike down some of the beef, I went around to both men and told them it was the Texas fever. They cut out the sick cattle, and each of them saved about half of their herds. If I had kept my mouth shut, they might have lost every head of beef."

"And your reward from Malcolm was to be given Sanson's place?"

"No," Zeke was quick to respond. "There never was any talk about Don's losing his ranch—nor being killed either. I was only going to have a free hand at the Vanderpool ranch, be allowed to pretty much do what I pleased. Part of the deal was a room of my own and no sleeping on the ground—a position I hadn't managed before in my whole life."

Roy considered Zeke's statement and believed he was telling the truth. However, it still left him with an unsolved murder.

"You've worked for Winston; what do you think of him?"

The old cowboy made a face. "He ain't much for grit, considering he has a pa like Malcolm. The boy has been browbeaten all his life. I 'spect if a train was coming and he was standing on the tracks, he wouldn't make the decision to move unless his pa told him to."

Roy sat at his desk and looked at his timepiece. He

had to meet Wilma Carmichael in a few minutes. Zeke seemed forthcoming, eager to do whatever he could to save himself a lengthy stretch in prison. As if thinking along those very lines, Zeke spoke up.

"Look, Sheriff, I know what I done was a bad thing, but I sure don't look forward to spending my last remaining days busting rocks with a hammer. You name what you want me to do, and I'll do it."

"Maybe something can be worked out," Roy allowed. "Cullen Lomax has some ideas. Let's wait and see what he has to say."

"You figure him to come back?" Zeke was incredulous. "Someone said the killer known as Concho had taken Miss Victoria."

"Yes."

"I've heard tell that that man is as cold-blooded as a snake." He pointed a finger at Roy. "Hey! I'll bet my eyeteeth that he's the one who killed Sanson. It'd be just the kind of thing he would do—one shot and ride away. I'll wager it was him."

"Could be," Roy acknowledged. "With luck, we'll know the truth when Lomax gets back."

"Sure hope he comes back as a mortal," Zeke said, rolling his eyes. "I'm not real fond of the idea of passing the time with ghosts."

"I'll be back in a little while," Roy told him. "You be good, and I'll bring you a decent meal from the hotel. You start making noise or giving me trouble, and you'll get nothing but bean sandwiches—without the beans."

"I'll sit right here and do nothing but pray for you to

have a kind heart and go easy on an old man who made a single mistake."

Roy made a face. "You spread too much of that kind of stuff around, and I'll have you cleaning the office with a shovel."

"Yes, sir, Mr. Sheriff. I'll be good."

Cully dropped Victoria off at the Melbourne ranch and told Jeff to meet him the next day. The sun had been down for an hour before he made it back to Elk City with the dead body of Concho. His first stop was at the jail. After tying off his mount and the second animal, he paused to remove the saddlebags from Ginger. When he pushed the door open, he saw Roy sitting on a chair next to a cell, with Zeke Pullman on the edge of the bunk inside. They were playing a game of checkers through the bars.

Both men turned as he entered. Zeke was agape with an expression of sheer disbelief, and Roy displayed a grin but also heaved a sigh of relief.

"Glad to see you made it, Lomax. How's Victoria?"

"I left her at the ranch. She was a little abused, tired, and hungry, but no permanent damage."

"How about Concho?" Zeke wanted to know. "I heard he was about as tough to kill as a Rocky Mountain tick—hit one of them with a hammer one time, and it bounced right off!"

"His body is strapped over his horse outside. I figured we would need to do some paperwork on him before planting his carcass in the boneyard."

Roy gave his head a bob. "I'm damned glad to see

you in one piece. Zeke has beaten me at checkers twice because I can't keep my mind on the game."

Zeke snorted. "That there's a better excuse than admitting I'm whupping the pants off him 'cause I'm the better player."

"Did Zeke here confess?" Cully asked Roy.

"He admitted to bringing in the Texas fever and infecting the two herds of cattle—the fever is passed to ordinary beef by ticks."

"What about Don Sanson's death?"

"I don't know nothing about that." Zeke spoke up for himself. "I told the sheriff here how I figure it was Concho who pulled the trigger, but I ain't got the slightest idea who hired him."

"We'll sort that out tomorrow," Cully said. "Roy, you need to set up a meeting at the bank—ten sharp in the morning. There's a list of people we'll need to have in attendance."

"I've got one to add to your list too." Roy got to his feet and explained about Wilma Comichael's arrival.

Cully noticed that the sheriff smiled a lot when he talked about the lady. Once he told Roy what he had learned, the sheriff reached over and patted him on the shoulder.

"Let's tend to Concho's body, and then you can get cleaned up and have something to eat. What do you want to do with the ransom money?"

"Leave it here in the jail. Zeke can keep an eye on it."

Zeke stood up, a surprised expression flooding his features. "You trust me to watch your money?"

"According to your story," Roy said, "you didn't mean any serious harm."

"That's sure enough the truth," Zeke vowed.

"Other than killing off a thousand head of cattle," Cully reminded him.

"Well, yeah, but I . . . ."

"And you claim you'll do anything to keep from going to prison?" Weathers asked.

"Sure 'nough, I'll do whatever you . . . well, 'most anything you want."

Cully walked into the second cell and dropped his saddlebags onto the bunk. "This is your chance, Zeke. I've got an idea in mind that might keep you from doing any time behind bars." He gave the old-timer a hard look. "However, if you have lied to us or try to double-cross us in any way, I'll hunt you down and kill you like a rabid dog."

"No! No!" he exclaimed. "You can trust me! I swear!"

"Someone comes in and tries to let you out or steal that money, you'd better let out a holler the devil will hear."

"You got it," Zeke promised. "I'll watch the office for you boys."

Cully and Roy left the jail together. Cully paused long enough to tell Roy what he had in mind, and the old sheriff nodded and said, "You name the tune, and I'll sure enough whistle along with you."

"Once we tend to Concho's body, you pass the word and see that everyone knows to be at the meeting,"

Cully instructed him. "After I finish up and have something to eat, I'll take over at the jail. You won't have to spend the night, because I'll sleep in the extra cell." He narrowed his gaze into a knowing look. "In fact, if you've got plans for breakfast, I can take care of Zeke until the meeting."

Roy's face brightened at the news. "That sounds like a good idea. I'll bring Wilma along, and we'll join you at the bank."

Malcolm Vanderpool's office was full. To one side of the room were Winston, Sandra Longmont, and her brother, Bud. On the other was Martha, Jefford, and Victoria Melbourne. Malcolm sat behind his desk, while Sheriff Weathers and Wilma Carmichael were seated by the door. Cully was the lone person in the room without a chair, but he was the one who would be doing most of the talking.

"All right, Sheriff"—Malcolm showed his impatience—"we are all present and accounted for. What is this all about?"

"I'll let my deputy handle this meeting," Roy said.

"The Melbourne handyman?" Malcolm grunted his contempt. "What the hell is this, a class on mending corral fences or something?"

"Cullen Lomax is an ex-Pinkerton operative," Roy explained. "His last job was as an undercover agent for nearly two years. He helped bring to justice a gang who specialized in stealing gold and silver, after infiltrating the operation and learning that the head of the group was a well-respected businessman who owned a smelter. The band of thieves would steal gold and silver from the express wagons, banks, or railroad. No one could trace the ore, because the head man was using the smelter as a cover and processing the ore along with the usual mining shipments. The Pinkertons and men from the Treasury Department moved to close down the operation, and Lomax was responsible for putting eight men behind bars."

Roy let the story sink in. "Jeff Melbourne is the only man in Elk City who knew about Lomax's past. The reason he hired him was to be more than a handyman. Jeff wanted him to look into the outbreak of Texas fever, which took half of both his and Don's herds. When Don was killed, and Lomax and Victoria were ambushed, Jeff came to me. Between us, we have sorted out some details and have a pretty good idea of everything that has happened."

Malcolm's haughty expression faded, replaced with one of concern. "You know who killed Don?"

Cully waited, but Roy turned the floor over to him. He took his first step to stand in front of Malcolm's massive desk and regarded the man with a steady gaze.

"We know you hired Zeke Pullman to infect the cattle with Texas fever," he stated emphatically. "Zeke told us how he figured out the fever was carried by ticks—ticks that do not harm a longhorn steer but will kill ordinary beef."

"I don't know what—"

"Hold your tongue, Vanderpool!" Cullen barked the

order. "We're going to arrest someone in this room today, and it just might be you!"

Malcolm tried to put on an indignant look but failed miserably. He swallowed his vanity and gave a reluctant bob of his head.

"You needed access to the river—either Jeff's northern pasture or Don's southern range. Your devastating their herds caused both men to borrow heavily against their ranches, something you thought would cause one of them to sell one of those properties, but it didn't work."

Cully paused a moment and continued. "That's when you decided upon a backup plan and coerced Mrs. Melbourne into accepting an arranged marriage between Victoria and Winston. With their ranch already in debt to finance Avery Melbourne's inn, they were not going to meet this year's mortgage payment. You offered a partnership, one she had to accept or risk losing the empire her father had built up from scratch."

"What is it you want?" Malcolm asked. "If you arrest me, I'll still own the Sanson place."

"No, you won't," Cully replied. "The Sanson place goes to the next of kin." He rotated and tipped his head toward the woman sitting next to Roy. "Mrs. Wilma Carmichael is Don's older sister. She has assumed ownership of the ranch."

The banker's jaw dropped, and he suddenly looked sick. "Don had a sister?"

"And there will be no wedding between Victoria and Winston, so you have lost everything you sought to gain."

He stared blankly. "By whose authority are *you* calling off the wedding?"

Cully didn't elaborate on that point. Instead, he stuck to the case against Malcolm. "You stand to be arrested and convicted of crimes that would put you behind bars for years."

Malcolm grit his teeth and clenched his fists, but he made no objection.

"If you're interested"—Cully used his leverage—"there is a way to settle this without your winding up in prison."

"I'm listening," Malcolm said softly.

"Return the deeds to Jefford Melbourne and Wilma Carmichael as restitution for their loss of cattle. As for the ransom, that five thousand dollars will help get Mrs. Carmichael's ranch back into working order." Malcolm opened his mouth to protest, but Cully silenced him by adding, "In return for the money, the new owner has agreed to sign over the south pasture to you—with the provision that your crew puts in a fence to separate the land, so as to prevent the two herds of cattle from mixing together. In essence, you will have gained what you desired from the beginning—access to the stream for your beef. If you agree to these terms, both you and Zeke Pullman will be spared lengthy prison sentences."

Malcolm endured a mighty inner but visible battle, one that caused blood vessels in his forehead to rise and colored his complexion a reddish brown. Rather than explode from the pressure, he cursed under his breath.

"It's blackmail . . . extortion!" he lamented. "Five

thousand dollars is ten times more than that southern pasture is worth!"

"I've calculated the loss of cattle, Mr. Vanderpool," Cully replied evenly. "Jeff owes much more on his place than Don, so returning his deed will about make you even. With Don's place, however, the cash money is to make up the difference on his loss. Mrs. Carmichael was kind enough to offer you the southern pasture as a measure of good will. If you wish to debate the terms of this agreement, we can settle this whole thing before a judge—after you and Zeke have been sentenced."

"You are standing with your foot on my neck!" Malcolm growled.

Cully put an icy stare on the man. "It's restitution or prison—the choice is yours."

"Take the offer, Father!" Winston pleaded. "I never knew how you managed to infect those herds, but I was sure you were behind it. You committed a crime, and this will rectify the situation. You don't want to go to jail!"

Malcolm pounded a fist on the desktop to vent his rage. After the short outburst, he took a deep breath and lowered his head in defeat. "Yes . . . yes, it's a deal. I'll return the deeds. The mortgages are expunged."

"Fine," Cully approved. "That takes care of one order of business."

"Wait a minute!" Jeff Melbourne spoke up. "You said Malcolm was after our ranches. If so, he must have been behind the murder of Don Sanson."

Cully gave his head a negative shake. "Even with the

failure of his first plan, Malcolm intended to gain access to water by virtue of the arranged marriage between Winston and Victoria. He had no reason to kill Don."

"Then, if he didn't order him killed"—Jeff expressed his puzzlement—"who did?"

Cully put his attention on Winston. "You didn't want to marry Victoria." He stated the fact simply. "Once Sanson was dead, you thought you would be released from the wedding, because your father would claim the deed to his ranch."

Winston licked his lips, a trapped and frightened expression clouding his face. "Yes," he answered uneasily, "that's what I thought. But his death didn't change a thing. Father still insisted on going through with the wedding!"

"I imagine you kept Sandra Longmont informed about the situation?"

Winston frowned. "We talked about it, yes."

"She knew your father's plans and ambitions . . . the fact that he would never let you out of the wedding."

"Well, I suppose she . . ."

Cully swung his gaze to Sandra. "You knew what Malcolm Vanderpool was like, didn't you?" he challenged. "The man came into Elk City like a black cloud and coveted everything within sight. Having access to the water would not be enough for a power-hungry man like him— not if he could gain control of the entire valley."

"You expect me to answer?" she asked, stunned by his directing his attack at her.

"Winston kept you informed of everything Malcolm did or wanted," Cully continued. "Isn't that the truth?"

The lady had grown pale, but she did not faint away under his verbal assault. "Yes, I knew how much Malcolm desired control of the valley. I don't see that it proves anything."

Cully studied her closely. "Winston told you," he repeated. "So who did *you* tell, Miss Longmont?"

"I don't know what you're getting at," she protested. "I'm not involved in any plot; I only wanted to marry the man I love!"

Cully scrutinized the honesty in her eyes, then quickly drew his gun and swung it about to cover Bud.

"When you and I had our little talk, you mentioned how your sister, Sandra, had suffered a hard life before you came to Elk City, Mr. Longmont," he said. "I recall your telling me how you've taken care of her ever since she was a little girl."

Bud glared at the muzzle of Cully's pistol but remained silent.

"What are you saying?" Sandra wailed. "You can't believe my brother had anything to do with Don Sanson's death!"

"Concho gave you away, Bud," Cully told the young man. "He told me I was never his target, that setting a second ambush for me was to get even for my killing his pal. That could only mean he was sent to kill Victoria."

"I told you about him!" Bud battled back. "I'm the one who warned you about Concho."

"Only because your sister confided in you that

Winston had finally found the backbone to tell his father he was not going to marry Victoria. You didn't want an innocent girl being killed for no reason."

Sandra turned to look at her brother with a mixture of horror and disbelief. "Bud," she pleaded, "tell him you didn't do this. Tell *me* you didn't do this!"

"I acted alone," Bud said firmly. "Sandra didn't have no part in this." He lowered his head with guilt. "I'm the one."

"Bud!" Sandra cried. "What are you saying?"

Her brother, unable to meet his sister's imploring look, spoke to Cully. "My sis ain't caught a break her whole life," he said. "Forced to do the cooking and keep our run-down shack like a full-grown woman before she was in her teens. She took in laundry and learned to mend clothing to help keep food on our table. She never got to be a kid, never had a chance to be a young lady, because she was too busy trying to help us survive. She owned one pair of shoes and two dresses when we moved here—it's all she has ever owned." He heaved his shoulders in a shrug. "When she met Winston, I figured she had finally had a turn of luck . . . until Malcolm decided to arrange a marriage for him and ruined everything."

"No!" Sandra sobbed. "Oh, Bud, I . . ." But she could not produce any words.

"Where'd you get the money to hire a man like Concho?" Cully asked. "He wouldn't have come cheap."

"From my sister," he admitted. "She borrowed some money from Winston. She told him it was to help me start up a business of my own. I let on that I was working on something big, and she never questioned me about it."

"Why did you have to kill Don?" Roy asked.

"Because he refused to sell the piece of property that would have given Malcolm's cattle access to the water. Both Jeff and Don held on tightly to their land and wouldn't give an inch. Don had lost his wife and had no family . . . well, that I knew of." He avoided looking at Wilma Carmichael. "With Don out of the way, I thought it would be enough to satisfy the greedy blood-sucker."

"But he didn't call off the wedding." Cully went forward with the story.

"No, it seems having Don's ranch was not enough to satisfy his lust for wealth and power. When Sandra came crying to me that Winston was still trapped into the arranged marriage, I . . ." He swallowed from the shame again. "I told Concho to . . ." But he could not finish.

"Sheriff." Cully spoke to Roy. "I believe you should take Bud here into custody. Because of the deal struck here today, Zeke is free to go."

Winston took hold of Sandra's hand. As Roy took Bud Longmont from the room, Wilma and the young couple followed.

Malcolm also rose to his feet. "I never thought . . ." he began. "Everything . . . this is all my fault."

"Greed can make sinners out of saints," Cully said. "You have your empire, but it won't be as big as you wanted."

"I'll get you those deeds," he said, his manner displaying remorse for having cost several lives. "It's time we put this entire affair behind us."

Cully holstered his gun and rotated to face Jeff, Martha, and Victoria. He presented himself to Jeff and removed his hat.

"Mr. Melbourne," he began, "it would give me the greatest honor of any man on this earth if you would allow me to marry your daughter."

"Jefford!" Martha cried. "I think we should discuss—"

Jeff raised a hand, and she broke off in midsentence. His gaze went not to Cully or his wife but rested on Victoria.

"I have to know your heart on this matter, dear daughter. What is it you wish?"

Instead of replying to him, Victoria cast a heated stare at Cully. "You might have had the decency to ask me first!"

Cully grinned at her. "Sparks, I figured the way you kissed me, you *did* give me the answer to that question."

"He will take a lot of grooming to ever amount to anything more than a handyman." Victoria now spoke to her father. "But I think I am up to the chore."

Jeff nudged his wife with one shoulder. "He did save our daughter's life," he told her gently. "And he is an ex-Pinkerton operative—hardly the worthless drifter you have believed all these months."

Martha scanned the faces of the other three and groaned. "I suppose we can proceed with all of the planning . . . with only a change of groom. I hate to think who might attend from Cullen's side." Looking up at him, she asked, "Do you know anyone other than criminals?"

"Roy and Wilma, the boys at the ranch . . . there's a couple of Treasury agents. . . ."

Victoria laughed as her mother groaned a second time. "Mother, I'll leave the wedding in your hands!" she exclaimed, jumping to her feet. She paused to flash a bright smile at the woman. "*I'll* make sure Cully doesn't stand me up at the altar."

Cully put his arm around Victoria's waist and headed for the door. "Now, am I allowed to kiss you publicly?"

"That's not proper for a lady—at least until I hear you utter the words 'I do' in front of a preacher, mister," she said with authority.

"Sparks, you're an amazing woman."

"You have no idea, Cully." She laughed. "But you will have the rest of your life to learn."

Cully pulled her close and smiled. "I'm looking forward to becoming an educated man!"

W